BLOOD MAGIC BLUES

HOP-D Case 1

P. A. WILSON

Free ebook

Claim your copy of Spells and Other Charms when you use the QR code to sign up for my newsletter and learn more about Quinn and Cate's past.

Chapter 1

Fernlight looked around the office space. Bramble was flitting from the corner of the desk to the bookshelf and back. Opening a business was risky; doing it as the first sprite private detective added a layer of uncertainty that human businesses didn't have. Partnering with a fairy would at least make it interesting.

Bramble settled for a moment on one of the client chairs. "When will our first customer come in?"

He was currently in his natural state, about three feet tall with visible wings. When he'd first approached Fernlight, she'd been reluctant to take on a fairy. They were short-lived and had short attention spans. But he'd convinced her that their goals were the same: to make a place in the human world. Bramble's clan had no power in the fairy world, and he was determined to change that.

"Client," she said. "They are called clients. And I don't know. We did what Dionne said; posted on social media and made a website. But that doesn't mean people will knock on our door on day one. Especially since it's almost closing time."

His eyes lost focus for a moment and a glamor slid into

place. Now the wings were gone, and he looked to be closer to five feet tall. "Now I'm dressed for business. And it's not my fault we had to wait for the furniture."

No, she'd been the one to order the desks and chairs. "I know."

"We need to make something happen," he said. "I don't have the time for us to sit around waiting. I need to make my name now!"

Fernlight sighed. "You've been reading those inspirational posts on Facebook again."

"Twitter; I think that's more fun," he said.

She couldn't argue his point. Sprites were long-lived beings — people; she must remember that they were now considered people because it made the humans more comfortable — so she was patient, but perhaps the business needed a boost. Perhaps their agency needed to be more like a fairy than a sprite right now.

"What about doing some networking?" she asked. "See if there are any business groups we could join."

He hopped the desk to sit in his chair. Bramble's desk was near the east wall and Fernlight's desk near the west. It looked open, but they had a privacy spell that could separate the two areas when needed. The desk was metal and glass, the chairs plastic, the floor terracotta tile. No wood was wasted on furniture.

"You look nice," Bramble said as he typed. Another annoying trait. He didn't always answer her question if he had something to say.

Dionne, Quinn Larson's apprentice and one of the six beings who brought about the prophecy, had taken up the challenge of helping Real Folk blend better with humans. She'd outright ordered Fernlight to get some business suits and work clothes. Sprites were more likely to spend their time in loose clothes when they weren't naked in the forest.

Fernlight smoothed the side of the dress she wore. It was moss green and matched her eyes. She would put on the jacket when they had a client, to increase the businessperson effect. The flat shoes were less uncomfortable each time she put them on; barefoot was another no-no. At over six feet tall she wouldn't need the added stature of heels, thank the spirits.

"Why would that work?" Bramble asked. He clicked the mouse and kept searching.

Dionne had explained this as well. Fernlight was getting used to repeating information to Bramble enough times that he remembered. It wasn't everything, and it was irritating, because if he heard something that interested him, he never forgot it.

"People will know us, and then when they have a problem, or a friend has one, they'll come to our agency."

"We could go for afternoon coffee with this mastermind group," Bramble said, turning the computer so she could read the screen.

"It says they are a knitting group." She pointed to the heading on the page.

"Does that mean they won't need something investigated?" Bramble sat with his fingers poised over the keyboard. "What should I look for? Do you think there's a group called, 'people who need private investigators'?"

Fernlight shook her head and moved to her own desk. The effort it took to answer Bramble's questions was much higher than the effort to do the research herself, even with her lack of skills. "Business people like us might be better."

"Why?"

Good question. This morning she'd felt optimistic, happy to start the business, looking forward to helping people find lost relatives, or catch someone doing wrong. But the *idea* of having a business was very different from actually running one. Despite her earlier words, she had held a tiny hope that someone would just walk in the door as soon as the sign was unveiled. The Magic Search Agency didn't need much clarification.

"I don't know," she said in answer to Bramble's questions. "What do you think?"

Bramble sat back in his chair. "I think we should try to meet as many people as we can. We don't know who will need our help. And it will be fun." The last words trailed off. Bramble, like most fairies, was afraid of humans. He'd sworn that it wouldn't get in the way, that he was going to be the first fairy who could handle humans, but there was still some trepidation in his voice.

"Hello." The front door opened, and a young human woman stepped into the office. "Are you open?"

Bramble froze, despite his efforts to overcome his fear. So Fernlight stood and reached out her hand to shake with this first client. "Yes, this is our first day. I'm Fernlight." She gestured to Bramble and introduced him. The woman shook Fernlight's hand and waved at Bramble.

"I'm Bella," she said. "I run the cafe next door? Vegan Victuals?" Every sentence was a question.

"How can we help you?" Fernlight said.

"Oh. No, I'm not here to hire you. I'm offering you help. We have a small business community group and we all try to help out." Bella smiled and then pointed at Fernlight's arm. "I love your tattoos, by the way."

Running her finger along her skin, Fernlight said, "That's my skin, not a tattoo." Unlike Bella, who had very pale skin that contrasted with her bright red hair, Fernlight had white hair that grew in short spikes and skin the color of Arbutus bark with faint grain lines.

Bella blushed. "I'm so sorry. I've never met a sprite before."

Fernlight pointed to the client chairs. "No need to apologize. Tell us about this community group."

As she turned to follow Bella, Fernlight noticed a man

standing outside the office, staring into the window. He looked angry and she hoped he was simply waiting for a friend, and not the first of a group of protesters. Some humans still wouldn't accept that magic was normal.

THE MAN WAS STANDING OUTSIDE.

Just like a human to be weird. Bramble turned away from his surveillance of the possible attacker and glanced at Fernlight. It was too hard to keep his thoughts on the human when his partner was sitting there with another one. He tried not to be afraid. He remembered what Fernlight said, that the humans were not going to hurt him. It did help a bit, but it was still hard to keep his eyes on both threats.

"When is the next meeting?" He heard Fernlight ask the female.

Were they going to a meeting with lots of humans? How was he going to keep them safe? He expected to have time to prepare for that. His heart fluttered, and the room began to spin.

Bramble placed his hands on the desk to stop the room spinning. If he couldn't manage one human nearby and one outside, Fernlight wouldn't let him be her partner. If that happened, his family would fade into the shadows of fairy life. His only chance to improve his standing with the other fairy tribes was to be the first to successfully work with humans face-to-face. To even help them.

Dionne had known what would happen. She worked with lots of fairies, so she knew how hard it was to not be afraid. Bramble closed his eyes and imagined how life would be for his grandchildren. It would use up his whole life to make them important; this was for the future. The happy image of a large tribe of Bramble fairies slowed his heart and steadied the room.

When he felt safe, he opened his eyes and let go of the desk. His heart sped up again.

The man was opening the door!

Bramble looked to where Fernlight was still talking to the female human. She gave him the look. That stare. The one that meant, this is your chance to prove your worth. Or maybe just meant, say hello and ask the man to wait.

Bramble poured a little more energy into the glamor, making himself an inch taller, then stood up and walked to the man.

"Welcome to the Magic Search Agency," Bramble said. He was proud that his voice didn't shake, but decided it might be better if it wasn't so squeaky. "What can we do to help you?" The baritone voice rumbled pleasantly in his chest.

The human took a step back. That was a surprise. Maybe he didn't like deep voices.

"I am Agent Bramble." This time it was a higher voice, but it gave the man twitches around his mouth. "Do you need something investigated?"

Now the human showed his teeth. Bramble took two steps back. The man was getting ready to eat him!

The man closed his lips. Perhaps he wasn't going to eat them yet.

"I am Mamoru Yamana," he said. "I want to engage your services."

Their first customer! Bramble felt his wings start to push through the glamor in his excitement. "Come to my desk. I will listen to your request and then my partner will join us."

The man looked at Fernlight and the woman then back at the desk Bramble pointed to.

"This is confidential," he said.

"Yes, come and tell me what you need," Bramble said, pointing again to his client seat.

The man shook his head. "I need privacy. I will return when you have no other clients."

No!

Bramble wanted their first client to be his. It didn't matter that it was a human. He wasn't scared anymore. He was excited. And Fernlight would know how valuable a partner he was.

"The other human will not hear us," Bramble said. Now his voice was too high, the man winced. He knew humans could only hear some voices, and fairies could hear and speak outside those ranges. He tried to calm himself. He looked around to see what the man saw. Oh no! He'd forgotten to put up the privacy spell. "Look," he said waving the spell into action.

The man raised an eyebrow as a wall of tree trunks appeared between the desks. Fernlight had chosen the appearance and refused to make it a wall of brambles when he made the suggestion.

"Come, sit, and you will see that we cannot hear them." Bramble wanted to pull the man to the chair, but he wasn't quite ready to touch a human.

The man stepped forward, not to the chair, but to the wall. He reached out to press his fingers against it, then pulled them back as they sank into the trees. "Impressive."

Bramble grinned and wanted to flit around the room, but he knew that would not be the way a serious agent would behave. "Sit. Let's get your information on the file."

His client pulled the chair out and sat.

Success!

While the human settled, Bramble opened a notebook and selected a pen from the twenty he had in his drawer. Each one was a different color, and he thought it would look good to have files in different colors too.

"Before we start a file," the human said. "I want to know more about your experience with investigations."

Bramble almost said, 'we don't have any' when he remembered that he was not supposed to say things like that. He was supposed to say things to make their customer... no no no, client... comfortable. They had talked about this because Fernlight said humans would want to be sure that they were hiring someone who would help.

"We use our special skills to find answers," he said. It didn't sound right to him. Was he supposed to be enthusiastic about it? It wasn't a lie, not that he had a problem with lying to humans, or anyone for that matter.

"How have you used those skills?"

Bramble's mind froze up. He'd said the words they'd agreed, and it hadn't worked. What should he say next? Maybe they should have made up a case so they could show how great they were at investigation.

Bramble could feel his glamor slipping as he struggled to think of an answer.

Then, the human woman walked past following Fernlight to the door. It felt like a lifetime, but as soon as they were alone, Fernlight canceled the privacy spell and sat beside the human.

FERNLIGHT JOINED Bramble and the human. As she did, Bramble's body stopped trembling and relaxed into his usual fidgety mode. At least this time he hadn't gone catatonic.

"I'm Fernlight," she said. "This is Bramble, we are the lead investigators. How can we help you?"

The man smoothed his suit and then placed his hands in his lap. His posture straightened even more. Fernlight had never seen a human sit so straight.

"I am Mr. Yamana. Mamoru Yamana," he said. "I believe I may need to hire you to solve a particular problem."

He didn't elaborate and Fernlight understood Bramble's reaction. They could follow their prepared scripts all day, but if the client wouldn't share, nothing would happen.

"If you can tell us a little?" She made it a question because she'd noticed that humans seemed compelled to answer questions.

"I require you to keep this confidential."

Fernlight gave Bramble a glance. He returned it with a glare as if there were no chance of him blabbing secrets.

"You have our word," she replied. "But if that is not enough, you can sign a client agreement, and then you'll have our liability." The online sales classes that Bramble had found suggested this as a closing tactic; get the client committed early.

Mr. Yamana tugged at his sleeves before speaking. "I would prefer we sign an agreement. It is not so much for me, but this case is too important to leave anything to chance."

Fernlight nodded to Bramble and he printed the form. This Mr. Yamana was taking a chance on them. It would not do to be offended by his professionalism.

When Bramble placed the form and a pen on the desk, Fernlight held out her hand to him. "The spell."

Bramble started and then blushed. "Sorry, I forgot." He opened a locked cupboard and pulled out a twist of parchment.

"Mr. Yamana," Fernlight said. "Signing the form is one level of protection for you. I am sure the humans would find that sufficient."

He nodded, but the wry smile told a different story.

"With Real Folk," she continued, "we can improve on that. This spell will make it impossible for us to discuss the case without your permission. Or by applying the oath to that person."

"Interesting," he said, tapping the pen against the paper. "What is required?"

The first hurdle over — most humans were still suspicious of magic — Fernlight opened the parchment. "We say these words and burn the paper and its contents. You will add a permission word at the end."

"Very well," he said.

"The form goes first," Bramble said. "It anchors the spell."

Fernlight placed her hand on the desk, their signal that Bramble should stop speaking. Without it, the fairy would likely go off on a tangent and tell four or five stories about similar spells.

Mr. Yamana signed and passed the form to Fernlight. When all signatures were completed, she placed the contents of the parchment in an ashtray and gave their very first client the script of the spell.

"Do you have a permission word? It should be something you wouldn't accidentally say, but not so weird that people would know something is up, and you could say it when strangers are around, and they wouldn't know you were doing anything, and it should be simple…"

His nerves were making him ramble despite her signals. Fernlight touched Bramble's hand. The fairy snapped his mouth shut.

Mr. Yamana's mouth twitched with a suppressed smile. "I will use the word, persimmon. It is in season, so it will not be odd to speak the word. I do not care for them, so I am unlikely to say it by accident."

When Mr. Yamana nodded that he was ready, Fernlight lit the small heap of herbs and twigs in the ashtray, and all three recited the spell. As soon as Mr. Yamana spoke his permission word, Fernlight took the parchment from him and tossed it on the embers of the ingredients. A sudden flame consumed the parchment and remaining ashes in a fire so hot it left nothing but a curl of smoke.

"I feel different," Mr. Yamana said. "As though I would know where you are even without seeing you."

Bramble picked up the ashtray and moved it to the side of the desk. "Yes, that is part of the spell. It will fade a little as time passes and we will undo it when the case is solved, and you won't need to worry, we are just connected now, and there's no…"

This time Fernlight stopped Bramble with a look.

She turned back to their client. "Mr. Yamana."

"Mamoru, please. We are connected so it seems impolite to use such formalities."

She nodded. "If you will tell us about the case, and why you chose us."

He unbuttoned his jacket and relaxed. The movement turned him from a stiff cold human to a friendlier, more open one. Fernlight tucked that knowledge away for use in the future. Human body language was still a gray area for most Real Folk.

"I think it will be apparent why I came to you, when I explain the case. But first, you must know that I work for the Human Occult Protection Department, in the investigation bureau."

Fernlight glared at Bramble to keep him from responding. HOP-D, as everyone seemed to call it, was supposed to protect both humans and Real Folk, but mostly it seemed to side with humans. "I would think you have all the investigative power you need."

Mamoru shifted in his chair. "It is not the power, but a difference of opinion on… shall we call it perspective? A case I was working on proved difficult, and despite the potential for severe damage to both humans and magical folk, I have been told to end my investigation."

"So, you came to us to keep your work going?" Fernlight

understood the rationale, but HOP-D would not let them simply look into a case they had deemed closed.

"Not exactly," Mamoru said. "I think I was close. I want you to find someone. If I can prove... Well, there are rumors of a drug that allows humans to do magic. If you can find proof, and one person who is using the drug, I can open the investigation again."

"And then HOP-D can blame us?" Bramble rose from his chair in indignation, his glamor slipping away.

Chapter 2

This was more than Fernlight had planned. Her first client was supposed to be easy; a lost pet, or a cheating spouse. A quick spell and then the agency would have some successes to use in marketing. That was what Dionne told them would be best. Now this man was asking her to work with an organization that had a reputation for blaming Real Folk for everything. And Bramble was beyond calming.

"I think we need to think about this," she said, keeping her eye on Bramble to make sure she could interrupt any explosion. "HOP-D is not what we envisioned as our first client."

Mamoru held up his hand. "I understand, but please let me be clear. I alone am your client, not my employer. I will be able to keep your involvement confidential."

He waited for Fernlight to respond. When she didn't, Mamoru stood. "When can I expect an answer? I must remind you of the urgency. If this drug is real, and it becomes popular, it will make the relations between humans and magical beings worse, not better."

Bramble was starting to sink back into the chair. His wings slowing to a blur of motion. "We understand. No human can simply take on magic and hope to survive. We will let you know tomorrow morning."

Mamoru didn't argue, but by the way his face had become expressionless again and his body rigid, he wasn't happy. He pulled a card from his pocket, held it in two hands to present to her. "I will wait for your call."

The back of the card faced Fernlight. A phone number printed across the blank space. When she flipped it over, the HOP-D logo seemed to jump out at her.

Fernlight watched until Mamoru was through the door and across the street. Bramble was still silent, but he had returned his glamor and was sitting in the chair, not floating above it. She was aware of the flicker of his heartbeat at the edge of her sprite senses; it was slower, but still fueled with emotion.

"We need more information," she said to forestall his immediate refusal.

"It's a trick," he grumbled. Then he started typing searches into the computer.

Fernlight would do a little magic research while Bramble used his skills in the electronic world. He'd surprised her with his skill when they'd learned of the internet. Perhaps it was his scattered fairy nature that made Bramble so capable with the computer. When she tried to do the same research, she found it too hard to discern real from fantasy.

"We can, at least, find out if Mamoru is telling the truth. And, perhaps, it is a trap for him, rather than for us."

"That won't matter," Bramble said without looking at her. "HOP-D will be happy to arrest Real Folk."

She sighed. There was no point in arguing until they had more facts. "I'll be right here." She pointed at the floor in front of the desk. The spell would work better if she was closer to where Mamoru had been. "I'll lock the door. If anyone comes, pull me out of the trance."

Bramble nodded, still typing rapidly.

Fernlight ignored her worries. She had agreed to partner with Bramble for a reason. She had to start trusting that he would take things seriously and not get lost in his research, emotions, or new interesting things that happened.

Fernlight kept a handful of the sunflower seeds that held the truth spell in her desk. Despite advice from the wizard who had sold them to her, she would not use them on humans without permission; it set a bad precedent. In the future, she'd make it part of the contract process. She'd been sure that any lie a human told would be easy to see. Now, she wasn't so confident.

Taking the matches and burn bowl from the desk, she lowered herself to the tiled floor. Dropping one seed into the burn bowl, she slipped into the light trance needed to focus her energy. It wasn't necessary to burn the seeds for the spell, but it made her feel better that no human could get them by accident and be hurt by any residual magic.

If Mamoru was right, then she needed to be far more careful. What if the drug worked, and then humans were able to pick up discarded spell ingredients? Even a trace of magic could cause damage in untrained hands.

Fernlight took the seed, held it tightly in her right fist and spoke the words of the spell. "If untruths have been uttered here, display them."

If Mamoru had lied, the words would float across the air.

Nothing happened.

When they'd stocked up on charms like this, Fernlight had expected that humans would be similar to Real Folk. That there was an underlying trust in the way the world worked. Now she knew it was naive to believe that. The lack of results didn't make her feel satisfied. It made her feel like they had been tricked. No matter what she said to Bramble, the mention of HOP-D stirred fear in her too.

She placed the sunflower seed in the burn bowl and lit the

match. It took longer than the contract spell to burn, and it filled the office with the odor of burned oil. When all that was left was ashes, she rose, opened the door and coaxed the air to blow a cleansing breeze.

Bramble was still tapping at keys, but now there were printouts on the desk beside him. By the light outside she had been in the trance for an hour. It was almost time to lock the door and leave.

"Any luck?" she asked.

He looked up. "Did he tell the truth?"

Fernlight confirmed the results of the spell. "What did you find?" She reached for the pile of papers.

"You want to take the case," Bramble said, staring at the screen.

Fernlight nodded. "It will be good for the business, but I want to hear your opinions. Bramble, we're partners. If you have a solid reason to say no, then we'll keep looking for another client. I just..."

He closed the lid of his computer. "I know. If we don't take it and the drug works, we'll be responsible for whatever happens."

And that was why she partnered with him. He got to the core of a problem fast. "We still have a choice. We can send Mamoru to the druids."

"Okay, but I thought you wanted to do this." Bramble fluttered to the chair beside her. "I thought I would be too afraid to take the case, but I think we should."

Surprised, Fernlight put the papers on the desk.

"I do, but I think there's more to it than what he told us. We don't know what the internal games are at HOP-D, we don't really know if there is a drug, just that Mamoru believes it."

Bramble waved his hand over the pile of printouts. "There's information in there that says the same as Mamoru, and more, and I don't know why they wanted him to stop the investigation, but I found all the details. The internet is full of things we need to know, and a little fairy magic opens all the files I need."

"So, we tell him yes?" Fernlight touched her middle where a tiny kernel of doubt sat hard and knotted.

"Yes, and we should do it now so we can get started, and he should come back, but I don't think he should know that I got all this. I think humans want to believe their secrets are safe, and I think it would work best for us, and all the Real Folk, if they kept thinking that. Do you want me to call Mamoru? I'm not scared to do it, and I can ask him if he will come back tonight."

Bramble's enthusiasm helped her to ignore the doubt. "I think we can wait until tomorrow to meet him. You go ahead and let Mamoru know we'll take the case and set up an appointment."

Chapter 3

Mamoru walked through the door at precisely ten as agreed on the phone. Fernlight appreciated his promptness; her nerves were almost as wound up as Bramble's. Now they could start working, and their business would feel more legitimate.

She gestured to the chair set in front of Bramble's desk and locked the door so that they couldn't be interrupted by anyone dropping in, and make their client more comfortable. She blew on the handful of chalk dust she held, and the windows became reflective to the outside. No one would be able to see what was going on inside, but everything outside was fully visible from inside the office. Another suggestion from Dionne to provide them with privacy.

Mamoru looked at the contract on the desk. "I will need to read this before I sign."

Bramble offered him a pen. "It is exactly what we agreed. If you think we can delay our investigation long enough for you to read it, that's up to you."

Fernlight's shoulders slumped. Now her partner had swung from terrified of humans to aggressive. Although, perhaps that was just a different form of fear.

"It will only take me a few minutes," Mamoru said, forestalling Fernlight's reaction.

He ran his finger down the page, turned the second and third pages quickly and then signed. "I assume you will start immediately."

"Yes," Fernlight said. "But we start with getting as much information as you have."

"I will send you the files I copied before the case was closed."

Fernlight took the contract from him. "I thought the case was just put on hold." She didn't know if a closed case would be better for their work or not. If they didn't have to dodge official investigators, it would be easier. But if the case was only on hold, there was always a chance that new information would open it again.

Mamoru pulled out his phone and touched a few images. "I've sent you a link to a shared folder. Please copy the files now, and then I will delete everything."

Bramble started typing. "You know it isn't enough just to hit delete. I can get a wizard to give you a spell that will remove all trace of the file forever. All trace except our copy, of course, that would be silly."

"I have a spell already."

So, it wasn't just magical detectives. Mamoru seemed comfortable with the whole magical world. "Does HOP-D use spell work on a regular basis?"

"No. It's not exactly against the rules, but neither is it considered acceptable detective work. That means I have to confirm with traditional methods anything I find with magic."

Fernlight's optimism faded; was there something else Mamoru had held back until the contract was signed?

"And if we can't find conventional proof that the drug is real? I think if we find the drug is simply a myth there is no need to prove it."

She watched Bramble start to lose his glamor. This time the entire image around his real appearance faded to translucence. Her partner might not like it, but they needed answers. HOP-D was not an organization to trust without checking.

"If we can find the drug, and the supplier, I will take it from there. I can easily find a way to 'accidentally' stumble upon evidence." Mamoru spoke quietly and kept his eyes on the desk in front of him. "I have done this in the past."

"Hired Real Folk to solve a case?" Bramble asked, his glamor fading further. "I thought we were the first, and we would be the only agency. I want to know who helped you!"

Fernlight patted the air to get Bramble to calm down. "Please tell us what you mean by that, Mr. Yamana." The use of his last name seemed to snap him out of a memory. Mamoru straightened and looked first at Bramble then at Fernlight. "I have not engaged any other agency. You are right. This is the first. I hope that this will be the beginning of a long and profitable relationship. One that may help to bring our peoples together."

Bramble sniffed and then recast his glamor, as though he'd just noticed it was gone. "You are hiding something. I can tell. I have a spell that shows when I am not hearing all of the things I need to hear. I don't like it and I don't trust you."

Fernlight saw pain cross Mamoru's face. "We do not need the details," she said. Then, regretting the words, she added, "If you wish to tell us, or you think it important, we will listen. We just want to know that we are doing this for the right reasons."

"Yes." Bramble said. "I need to know you aren't trapping us into making things worse, that you won't blame all the Real Folk and put us in prisons, or kill us — or worse."

Mamoru stood and straightened his jacket. "I assure you that my intention is to help both humans and magical folk. But I see, despite your words, Fernlight, that you need to know something that I hold close. A shame on my soul that I wish to keep secret. I cannot simply tell you. There are items I must bring from my home. I will return after my work is finished." He nodded his head in a tight bow and asked for the door to be unlocked.

When they were alone, Fernlight turned to Bramble. "A spell that tells you when you are not hearing all the things you need to hear?"

He shrugged. "I'm practicing my lying. I think we will need to do it when we are investigating. I expected only to use it on the villains, but now I see it isn't always clear who the villain is. Humans are so complicated. I did well though, right? He believed me and maybe we could get that spell, it would help a lot and save us time, and make us always successful in our cases."

Fernlight shook her head and removed the privacy spell on the windows.

"Well?" Fernlight asked. She needed time to absorb the new information, time that could be filled with Bramble's panic and babbling.

"We need to know his secret first," Bramble said in a perfectly reasonable tone. "This is still our first case, and we need it to be successful. I can't let my family down."

His words shocked the fuzz out of Fernlight's brain. It was embarrassing to have a fairy be the reasonable one in the relationship. "What could be so bad that we would have to say no?"

Bramble's eyes glazed over and Fernlight waited while he sorted through the multiple bad options. At least he kept this from happening every time there was a block to their progress. At the beginning, he'd spiral out of control when asked if he wanted clover honey or wildflower.

"He could have a secret prison where he keeps fairies in the dark, so they fade away, and then he collects their wings and grinds them to dust, and then he uses that dust to make himself feel like one of us so he can find the fairy treasure." He ended with a triumphant smile.

"How likely is that?"

"I don't know enough about humans to guess." Bramble shrugged and then smiled again. "Maybe he is going to say he is a wizard! That would be a huge secret for someone in HOP-D."

Fernlight smiled. Succeed or fail, this partnership was entertaining. "Did you sense any magic around him?" She hadn't sensed any, but she hadn't thought to look.

"No, but maybe he has a conceal spell?" Bramble started typing on his keyboard. Fernlight knew this meant that the subject was closed as far as he was concerned.

She wasn't done with it. Inside she wanted both. She wanted to avoid being involved with HOP-D. She wanted to solve the case because it was right there in their laps and no one else was walking through the door. And she knew that any case they were involved with would mean bad people. Humans had a wide range of things they would do to each other. The Real Folk were scheming too, but usually in political ways. Trying to gain prominence for their people or clans, rather than personal gain. Would contact with humans change that?

"Bramble, stop avoiding the conversation and help me think it through." She waited as he tapped his final few keys, then gave a heavy sigh and an eye roll. "If we make the wrong decision here," she continued. "It could be the end before we even have a chance."

Bramble rested his elbows on the desk, clasped his hands together, and rested his chin on them. "What do you want to talk about?"

Fernlight turned the monitor around and pushed Bramble's hand away when he reached to turn it back.

"I knew it," she said staring at the screen. The face of a

human man, kindness on his face, elbows on a desk, chin resting on clasped hands. The site's name: *having-difficult-conversations.com*. "We are not having a difficult conversation. We are discussing a case; making a business decision."

"Well, that's difficult for me." Bramble tossed his hands in the air and flitted above the chair.

Fernlight wanted to be stern, but he was trying, and he was truly confused. She felt the laughter rise through her body and burst through the fear and annoyance. When the laughter subsided, she sat across from Bramble. "I'm sorry. I don't want you to find this difficult. We'll need to be able to talk about cases when we don't agree."

"I was looking at how humans behave," he said, floating back to sit in the chair. "If we are going to solve their problems, we need to know how they think."

"Yes, we do. But if we are going to be different from other detectives, we have to act like ourselves." Fernlight felt the tension leave her body as she realized the truth of her words. "And we need to agree that we both have good ideas."

Bramble fairly glowed with joy. "Deal!"

"Then we'll do as you said, just wait to hear what his secret is before deciding." They would be cautious, but they needed the work.

MAMORU RETURNED JUST as the other businesses around them started to close. Bramble wondered if every day would be the same. They opened their doors and then closed them with only one person coming in. It would be good in a way. He was starting to get used to Mamoru, but another human would mean starting all over again; he wasn't sure how much his nerves could take. Even reminding himself that it was for the future of his clan didn't scare away the fear.

"If you would give us privacy again," Mamoru asked Fernlight.

Bramble waited patiently, only a slight flutter of his wings disturbed the glamor. Mamoru held a bag, and the objects inside were his secret, or part of it. Bramble could feel the layers of emotion coming off the man; shame, worry, and hope.

"What do you have to show us?" he asked, unable to wait for Mamoru to settle on the chair.

"I will tell you in a moment," Mamoru said, placing the bag on the desk. "First, I need to understand what you know of human history."

Bramble let Fernlight answer the question. It was easier for him to research on the computer if he just listened. And he didn't know much about humans anyway. Up until the prophecy, fairies had avoided them.

"You have a bloody history. Many wars. Sometimes taking on allies who were enemies, just so you could gain a short-term advantage," she said. "I think you have caused most of your strife by your own actions."

Mamoru nodded and looked at his hands. "Succinct, but true. Do magical folk not war?"

Fernlight glanced at Bramble. He didn't know why. The answer was no. Unless there was some history he didn't know.

"Only in our distant past. Now, we generally get along. The sidhe have internal strife, but it does not usually include the other folk." She looked at Bramble again, frowning.

He kept quiet because that's what she usually meant by stern looks. Probably she didn't want him to say all the bad things the sidhe would like to do to the fairies.

"And do people sometimes do things they regret; things done under compulsion?"

Mamoru reached into the bag, but didn't pull anything out. Bramble was ready to drag out the contents himself.

"Things done under compulsion do not carry any blame. The blame lies with whoever laid the spell," Fernlight said.

Mamoru pulled out a jeweled chain, too large for a bracelet. Perhaps a human necklace. The rubies and sapphires were spaced evenly along the chain. He counted to fifty and there were still more. Bramble's hand reached for it, then he pulled back. No matter how shiny it was, the pretty thing belonged to their client.

"This is a rosary. Very ornate, but it is a prayer device for one of our religions. I keep it to remind me of the day I helped to kill two people for no reason." He placed it on the desk and reached for the other object: a shoe.

Fernlight gasped.

Bramble looked from the shoe to the man sitting across the desk. "That's a nymph shoe."

Mamoru nodded. "I found it in the ashes of the fire a few days after the prophecy."

Fernlight reached out to the shoe, hands trembling. "No one died in that fire."

Bramble watched her reaction. She was supposed to be the sensible one and if Fernlight was going to get emotional, Bramble would have to be sensible. He wasn't sure if he could carry that off.

"That is what I've been told. I keep it to remind me what could have happened." He pushed the shoe closer to Fernlight. "I hope that no one did, but if you know otherwise..."

She shook her head and the trembling stopped. Bramble almost flew with relief.

"We would have missed someone; there are not that many nymphs." She pushed the shoe back to Mamoru. "You said two people. Was this one?"

Mamoru sighed deeply. Bramble could feel the pain roll off him in waves. He straightened his shoulders and looked at Fernlight. "It is a relief that I only have two deaths to carry in my heart. The other was Randall Bluth. I was part of that mob. Even though I was not the only one, I feel as though the deaths were at my hand."

Bramble remembered hearing from his mother about the time of the change. It was chaotic and dangerous, but the Arch-druid, Trahaearn, had made the world safe. At least, safe enough for people to walk around and start businesses. "You were all under the influence of Kali," he said. "It was not you; it was her. She used your bodies to do her work."

"I was weak enough to let her do that," Mamoru said, rubbing his face with both hands. "She didn't take over everyone's mind."

"It was not weakness," Fernlight said, touching Mamoru's hand. "Kali took opportunities, and some she manufactured. We are lucky she was replaced by Arianrhod as the goddess of fertility and death. You are not to blame."

Mamoru pulled on the official attitude as though it was a glamor. "I brought these for a reason, and it was not for you to forgive me. Or not in that way. If you will still work for me on this case, I would like to start. I understand if you wish me to step away, but this case is vital to both our worlds."

"We will work with you," Bramble said, surprising himself. This was a human and instead of fear, Bramble felt compassion.

"We need your permission to share the information with some people who might help us," Fernlight said. "The oath allows it if the person takes the same oath, but I would feel better if you said it was allowed."

Their business was a success! Bramble stilled his fluttering. Excitement wasn't professional.

Chapter 4

Fernlight knocked on the painted wood door of Heath's basement apartment. To say it was painted was an exaggeration, more paint peeled than stuck. It looked like Heath's fortunes hadn't improved with the advent of the new world. For most wizards, it was easy to make money with the small charms and spells the humans wanted. Heath had bigger ideas. And that made him the right person to involve in the case.

"Heath," she called, leaning against the wood, hoping to hear footsteps. "It's Fernlight. I called you. Remember?"

From the side of the house, she heard Bramble call out. "It's Bramble, too. Come open the door."

Fernlight stepped to the side of the house. Bramble was peering in a window. "Can you see him?"

Bramble flitted back to her. "I think he's in a back room. There's light and maybe something moving."

She didn't remember Heath being this absent minded. She pulled the phone from her pocket and dialed.

"This is Heath. You've reached me at a bad time. Leave a message and I'll call you back. Or if this is Fernlight or Bramble, come on in. The door is open."

Rolling her eyes at his naivety, Fernlight reached for the door handle. It turned and the door opened an inch. Then it was jerked from her hands as Heath appeared in the doorway.

His short blond hair stood in spikes, held up by sparking motes and a few twigs. He looked up at Fernlight and grinned. "You made it!"

"You look like you've been digging tunnels," Bramble said. "Can we come in?"

Heath stood aside and waved his whole arm in invitation to enter. "Of course. We can't conduct business in the doorway."

Inside it looked chaotic. Books, bowls, and vials were scattered across every flat surface, including the floor. Fernlight stepped carefully through the debris, for the first time wishing she could fly above it like Bramble.

"Is this normal?" she asked.

Heath looked around and grunted. "No, it's usually not this tidy."

For anyone but a wizard, the mess would have been a distraction. The few wizards of Fernlight's acquaintance resided in various ranges of mess. Perhaps if he was too busy to keep his house ordered, then Heath was doing better than she thought.

He cleared a chair and offered food.

"No," Fernlight said. "I think we should get down to business."

"I'd love some honey," Bramble said at the same time.

"Let me get some. It will only take a moment." Heath rushed into the room behind them.

Bramble landed on the stool beside her, shifting two books for room. "I'm sorry," he mumbled when he noticed her glare. "I'm hungry."

Fernlight didn't respond. Heath rushed back into the room with a saucer holding a small puddle of honey and a tiny spoon. "I hope this is okay," he said, handing the saucer to Bramble. "Now, this case, what is it?"

Bramble was slurping honey, so Fernlight said, "Before we give you details, you need to know you'll be bound by a confidentiality spell."

"Of course, go ahead."

Fernlight led the ceremony and then waited for Heath to open a window or cast a spell that would dissipate the smoke. He did nothing. She was not a wizard, but that seemed like bad methodology. She told him about the case and Mamoru, leaving out the information about his past. That was Mamoru's pain to carry.

"So you need spells to help," Heath said when she finished.

"You aren't worried about HOP-D?" Bramble asked with a squeak of surprise.

Heath shrugged. "I don't know if their reputation is just rumor, or if it's real. We'll make sure we're protected. If we solve the case, they may be happy, or not."

"Will you help us?" Fernlight asked. She didn't like talking about HOP-D, but she agreed with Heath; there wasn't much to be done about it.

Heath leaned against the wall, knocking a small shelf askew and tipping the tiny bottles on it to one side. He moved a step away and straightened the shelf. "That was close."

Fernlight looked at Bramble, hoping he'd jump in with questions to prompt Heath back to the subject. But Bramble was deeply engrossed in his honey. "Will you?" she asked.

He blinked at her as if he'd been in a trance. "Oh, yes, but I want to be part of your agency."

"You want to investigate?" There was no business to share right now, except this one case.

Heath laughed. "No. Oh my, I would be horrible at it. No patience, you see." He picked a few twigs from his hair and placed them in his pocket. "I want to be your expert. If you need wizard magic, you come to me. I want a share of the fees."

Fernlight wondered at the relief she felt that Heath did need money, that his appearance and home were not a cover for some other image. "What if you can't help?"

"I'll find the help we need." He opened his arms wide to encompass the whole room and the mess. "I am working on something important and I need to buy some equipment and ingredients. Now that we can interact with humans, I can do so much more with my magic."

Bramble looked up from the saucer. "Are you creating a drug to give humans magic?"

Heath laughed again, this time losing his breath. When he was under control, he said, "Your case would be solved if I was. No. Whoever is doing this is crazy. Giving humans magic would bring only trouble to us. My partners are less dangerous. They want to profit from magic." He paused and looked at the ceiling. "Of course, I may be underestimating their moral compasses. Some humans are very good at hiding the fact they have moral corkscrews instead."

"Ten percent of our fees," Fernlight said. There was no way to discuss it with Bramble before bargaining, but she knew the money was just a measure of success for him.

"Fifteen," Heath said. "And I want to be able to use your clients in my research."

His words were worrying, but Fernlight knew Heath didn't want to actually use the clients as subjects. "Twelve, and I need to know what you mean by use our clients."

"Maybe they will have access to things I need, maybe they will finance the research, maybe they will advise... I can't be more specific than— Oh, you mean will I harm them? No." The realization seemed to sober him. "I'm hurt you would think that."

Fernlight looked at Bramble. The fairy nodded and went back to licking the last smear of honey from the saucer. "We have a deal."

Heath led them through the adjacent room into a small windowless space and set wizard light glowing in the four corners. This room was clean. Not only of clutter, but also of magic remnants. Fernlight could sense the earth beneath her, but that was it. Heath kept his workspace pristine; a good sign for their partnership.

"Sit," Heath said. "I'll set the wards and then we can do some seeking." He took a roll of string from his pocket. "This is the best thing ever. Humans have inspired us to wonderful efficiencies. The string is soaked in salt and oil. It unrolls and forms a basic circle. When it's getting depleted, the color changes. Marvelous, right? This is only one of the things my business partners suggested."

Fernlight nodded, although sprites didn't use salt for protective circles, she'd sat through too many ceremonies where the salt circle took longer than the spell. If it worked, it was a bonus.

Rather than unroll the string as he walked the perimeter, Heath unrolled the entire spool, twirled it above his head, and let go. He watched as the spinning circle lowered to the ground and formed a protective ward. "Perfect," he said, as he pinched the ends together.

As soon as the two ends of the string met, the air thickened. Fernlight glanced at Bramble, who was enraptured by the whole thing.

"Do you have more of these kinds of spells?" Bramble asked, his eyes glowing.

She would have to speak to him about exercising a bit of control when he found out how to buy these efficient spells.

"They aren't spells," Heath said. "More like tools. You have to be careful, not all of them work, and some of them are downright dangerous."

"We need a place to start on the case," Fernlight said. "The sooner we start, the less chance that it will hit the streets."

Heath nodded his head and settled beside them. "You said there's no proof that the drug is real?"

"Yes," Bramble answered. "Mamoru, that's our human client, I'm not afraid of him by the way, he said that his organization doesn't believe the drug exists, but he knows it does, but can't prove it, so that's our job, to get him proof to open the case again."

Heath started pulling items from his pockets. Fernlight saw an acorn, a ball of small seeds, and a wad of bracken. Heath poked at the items for a moment and then looked up at Fernlight. "Are you sure that HOP-D can be trusted with the truth?"

She'd avoided thinking about that since Mamoru told them about his employer. Heath's question prodded her to stop dodging the doubts. "No. I don't think they can be trusted with anything. I think we need to find the drug maker and stop them, whoever they are."

Bramble floated a few inches from the floor in surprise. "What? That's not what I thought we were doing. Aren't we supposed to do what the client wants and then move on? What happened to that? You said when we started that we shouldn't get involved in the case more than what the client wants. But, yes, I see now. You are right. HOP-D won't destroy the drug, they'll use it. Maybe that's why they stopped the case, maybe they know who the drug maker is, and they are protecting..." his words were cut off as he hit the top of the dome of protection.

"So, we're agreed?" Heath said. "We do what it takes to stop this drug from spreading?"

Fernlight swallowed her fears and agreed. "Let's not tell

Mamoru until we have to," she said to Bramble, who was now sitting back on the floor.

Heath pushed the bracken bundle into the center of the circle, tucking the seed ball back into his pocket. "I'll start by sending out a general enquiry. Don't worry, no one will be able to trace it back to us. If the recipient knows something, they will forget we asked as soon as they respond. If they don't know anything, it won't linger more than a moment in their mind."

"What if they don't respond? What if someone has information and withholds it?" Fernlight knew in her heart that knowledge of the drug could be considered power. If a sidhe had knowledge... well, they lived for power.

"I can't add a compulsion to the spell." Heath placed his hand over the bracken. "I can add a marker that will tell us if anyone is withholding information."

"That will be better than worrying," Fernlight said. "Go ahead."

Heath pressed the bracken flat onto the floor and held it down while he spoke the words of his summoning. Fernlight heard only murmuring, wizards didn't like to share their spells with anyone.

He stopped speaking and pulled his hand away. The bracken bounced back into a wad, and then tendrils of magic rose to swirl in the air. The magic filled the dome of protection, and suddenly an image appeared. It flickered in and out rapidly. It was a man, perhaps a wizard, perhaps a human.

Fernlight kept her focus tight on the image and started to notice details. Not enough to identify him, but red hair would help. She also noticed that the flickering wasn't just the same image. In one flash the man was dressed in a suit and laughing. In the next, he was screaming and dressed in blue flames.

She leaned in closer; the image disappeared.

Then the tendrils of magic swirled back into the bracken and the circle was clear. Fernlight looked around her. Heath was wide-eyed and holding his breath. Bramble was lying on the floor. Her heart clenched, she reached to touch his shoulder. Under her fingers her partner was trembling, so not dead. Her heart beat again.

"I guess we know it's real," Heath stuttered the words.

"Yes," she said.

Chapter 5

Fernlight sucked in a deep breath to clear the fear and shock from her mind. The air tasted stale and smelled of rotting leaves.

Bramble shook himself and then sat up. He blinked and rubbed at his face, all while trembling. "What did I miss?"

It was good that he pulled himself together quickly, faster than either Fernlight or Heath. Perhaps they recognized the sheer horror of what would come of this more than the fairy.

"What did you see?" Heath asked. "Before we try to understand the meaning, we must agree on the facts."

Bramble shuddered. "Evil. I didn't know it really existed. I heard humans talk about it, but now I know what they mean."

"A human, I think," Fernlight said, knowing that evil was part of the meaning, but not what Heath wanted. "The face flickered, so I couldn't be sure. There was fire and pain, and the next moment there was normal. Or what I think was supposed to be normal."

"Magic," Heath said. "I saw magic come and go through the man. It was a human. I would have known if it was a wizard."

Fernlight closed her eyes to concentrate on the memory. As much as her mind revolted at the idea of reliving it, this was the job they'd agreed to do. "Could it have been possession? Like the vampires?" Five years ago, the Arch-druid had uncovered the fact that Vancouver's local druids had been possessed by the spirits of vampires. He'd won the battle to restore them. Even now, some of them were weak from the ordeal.

"Would that be better?" Bramble asked. "If this is a magic spell, we can, maybe, if we are lucky, find it and stop the production. If it's a possession, we don't know how to make that go away. And even if we did, whoever possessed this man could go on to another and another." His voice reached a pitch where Fernlight could no longer hear him.

She reached to touch his arm, trying to calm her partner down. "It means we do things differently," she said, keeping her voice even and soothing. "We will stop it."

Heath wiped sweat from his face and shook his body like a wet dog. "Right. I guess we need to find out if we're dealing with a spell or a possession," he said. "That's the first step. Then?" He looked at Bramble and then to Fernlight. "What about this client?"

Fernlight didn't care that Mamoru wanted to keep the magic out of the case. If he didn't like it, then she'd take care of this problem alone if necessary. "We need to check in with him and give a progress report. He'll be okay with us taking the next steps."

"It's not like HOP-D can fix it anyway," Bramble said.

She nodded and then stood. "How can we be certain about the drug or possession. I don't want to go back to Mamoru without facts."

Bramble flitted up to meet Heath and Fernlight eye to eye. "We know some things. One, it is real. Two, it's a human... although are we sure on that? It could be a Real Folk who made a mistake. It could be anything. How will we know?" He looked back and forth between Fernlight and Heath.

"We all saw the same thing," Fernlight said. "It felt human. I can't see why one of the Real Folk would take a drug for magic. If it was to increase magic, they could do so much safer, and more reliably. It only makes sense that it's a human."

"It smelled like human," Heath said.

Fernlight frowned at him. "There were no odors."

Heath bent to start rolling up the salt string. "Smell isn't the right word, but it's all I have. Humans have a smell... or a feeling... or something. I could be blindfolded in a crowded room and tell you how many humans are there."

"Can you tell which humans? If you could, then we could just go walking around sniffing until we came across the right human. But I guess that's going to take a long time, I mean, he might not even live here, we might have to walk all over the world. No, I can see that's a bad idea." Bramble had flitted to the door as soon as the protective spell broke.

Fernlight followed her partner into the front room, which now looked worse in comparison to the casting room. "We'll tell Mamoru what we saw. We'll tell him what we think, and we'll tell him we're going to keep looking until we can stop it."

Heath picked up an old book that carried a strong musty odor. "I'll see what I can find in the library. I might have to talk to the druids, but if someone made the drug, they had to start somewhere."

"What about possession?" Bramble asked, uncharacteristically brief and calm.

Heath put the book down and chose another. This one seemed to squirm when he touched it. "I think we can apply logic. The vision showed that this person experiences normality still, even if it's sporadic. Is that what we all saw?"

Fernlight nodded. This aspect of wizardry annoyed her, but often taking a professorial approach brought clarity.

"Then," Heath continued, "it must be a drug. Which of the Real Folk would be able to fight a possession? No matter how strong-willed, a human would be overwhelmed in one step. The possession would be complete and they would know nothing."

Remembering Mamoru's confession, Fernlight had no argument. "Then we look for the manufacturer." Her shame at the knowledge that it could be one of the Real Folk drained her voice of any confidence.

Chapter 6

Bramble stared at the telephone. All night he'd been building his courage to make the call. Fernlight was convinced that he needed to practice his dealings with humans. She wasn't swayed by his argument that he'd botch it out of fear. She'd told him to practice and that he didn't have much to say. And she'd promised to be sitting there ready to take over if... No! Think positive! He could do this. Mamoru was a good human. He'd sat right there across the desk and nothing bad happened.

He dialed the number.

"Human Occult Protection Department, how may I direct your call?"

Bramble slammed the phone down.

He hadn't practiced this. HOP-D! He'd forgotten the number went to their offices. They needed to get a separate number for Mamoru. The number on his card was his work number. Did they already know that a fairy had called? Were their enforcers on the way to take him from his family?

"What's wrong?" Fernlight asked.

Bramble turned to look at her, but all he saw was the top of the cabinets. He was at the ceiling again. He'd lost his glamor and his wings were beating fast enough to be invisible.

Calm… Calm… Calm… The mantra was working. He floated down and landed on his chair. Looking down he saw the glamor fade in and make him look like a human.

"HOP-D answered the call."

"What number did you dial?" Fernlight reached for the business card.

Bramble pointed to the first line. "Office number," he said, his voice shaky, and he could see his hand trembling.

She turned over the card. "This one." She pointed at a handwritten number. "Remember it's his personal phone."

"I forgot." He grabbed the card and dialed while the happiness of avoiding HOP-D filled him.

"Hi, Mamoru? It's Bramble, we have a report. Oh…" He shrugged and hung up.

"Is he busy?"

"No. It was his voice mail system."

"So, why did you hang up?"

Bramble looked at Fernlight. *Is she being crazy?* "I didn't practice leaving a message."

She laughed, and it made him laugh too, but he wasn't sure why.

"You did leave one," she said. "Now we wait for him to call back. Honey?"

Bramble nodded. Maybe it would all be that easy. He hadn't practiced but he'd left a message, and he was shocked when he did it, and still a little scared about the HOP-D call.

Fernlight placed the serving of honey on his desk, the scent of lavender tickling his nose, and the phone rang. Bramble really wanted the honey. He looked at Fernlight and she just pointed to the phone.

"Magic Search Agency," he said, eyes still on his food.

"It is Mamoru."

Bramble took a deep breath and then told the client what they'd agreed to say. "It is real. We will look deeper."

It was short and to the point. Bramble's tongue really wanted to add more information. To tell Mamoru about the horrible colors, the screaming, the image changing from normal to terror.

"Do you know who?"

Bramble looked at Fernlight for help. He'd forgotten everything. She reached and pressed the speaker button.

"Mamoru, this is Fernlight."

"Are you sure we will not be overheard?"

"The privacy spell is in place."

How could she sound so calm? Bramble decided he would observe and emulate his partner. If he was going to make this successful and give his family status, he'd have to act more like a sprite and less like a fairy.

"Do you know who?"

"Who is taking the drug, or who is making and selling it?" Fernlight asked. Bramble thought they were perfect questions.

"Any of it. If you give me a name, or can describe the person, perhaps provide an image through a spell?"

Bramble tried to match Fernlight's demeanor. "We didn't see enough to do the spell." He clamped his mouth shut before anything else spilled out. It didn't feel good. Like an itch he couldn't reach.

"Pity. Well, if you can give me something to take to my superiors, I can, at least, prove the problem exists."

"We could do that," Fernlight said. "But, how are we to know that HOP-D will stop this drug? It seems to me they are more likely to exploit it than destroy it."

Mamoru sighed. "My organization has a bad reputation. I admit there is enough history to indicate that HOP-D is biased toward humans. It is only a few people, and I assure you that we are rooting them out."

"That will only help when it's done," Bramble said. "But it's not and, right now, we don't trust them." *They do bad things, and they'll arrest us, and we'll disappear, and my wife and children will die, and no one will care.* It helped to think all the rest of the words.

"We are considering ways to change our reputation," he said.

Fernlight held up her hand so Bramble would let her take over; he remembered agreeing to it. If he wanted to take over a conversation, he would do the same, but right now, he wanted to talk about how they would change the way the Real Folk thought about HOP-D.

"We need to deal with today's reality," Fernlight said. "The best way to make sure this drug is taken off the streets, and the person who created it is punished appropriately, is for us to do it."

"We have laws. I am not comfortable agreeing to vigilante justice." Mamoru's voice was more clipped than usual. Bramble wondered if he feared retribution for the events in his past. Real Folk wouldn't do that; they understood possession.

"How would you punish this person? I am ashamed to admit that they are possibly not human. How would HOP-D ensure this wizard or druid would not simply create another drug?" Fernlight was full of excellent questions.

Another sigh. "Can we agree to discuss punishment when we find the culprit?"

"I can live with that," Fernlight said, she looked at Bramble, and he nodded. "Unless it's necessary to act without conferring with you, we will contain the culprit, and talk about punishment when that is done."

"Keep me updated," Mamoru said. "Every day, even if you

have nothing to report. If there is anything I can provide you, ask. Do not be flagrant with magic. It may complicate things later."

The phone went dead.

Chapter 7

They had left Heath puttering around his home. Fernlight was sure he would continue until he had answers. She knew Bramble wouldn't sit all day waiting, or digging around on the internet. It didn't sit well with her either; idling and letting someone else do the work. They were a detective agency, not a sitting around waiting agency.

"It's dark out," Bramble said. "We should go."

His lack of rambling startled Fernlight. She turned to look at him while she zipped up the jacket she'd borrowed. He usually had a little sparkle, but now his face was ashen, and shadows ringed his eyes. His hair hung limp, and he stooped. "What's wrong with you?"

A smile big enough to show most of his pointed teeth broke over his face. "It worked!"

He let the glamor slip away and Fernlight realized the shock of seeing him look so ill had made her miss the fact that his wings were not visible. Her partner stood before her now in all his fairy glory, looking as healthy as ever. "Where did you get that?"

They wanted to pass as much as possible as humans, so no magic casting to stop the glow. She had a generic human glamor on; it only sipped at the power, so it wouldn't need to be replenished. A glamor like Bramble's would take constant drips of magic; each one generating a spark.

"Heath," Bramble said, pulling something from his pocket. "Look. It's just a pine nut, it sits in my pocket and casts the glamor. If I want it to stop, I just cover it with my hand. I don't have to do any magic, Heath said it would last a whole day without needing a recharge. I thought I should kind of blend in. If we are going to the bad side of town, to alleys and maybe talking to drug dealers and users, I should look like I fit in."

It was a good idea, just one major flaw. "So, if you fit in, does that mean you'll talk to these humans? All by yourself?"

"Maybe," Bramble said the word so quietly that Fernlight almost missed it.

"Let's see what happens," she said, taking pity on him. "It's a good idea and maybe I'll get something from Heath the next time we meet."

Right now, they needed information, any kind of information. That's why they were going out and walking around the streets at night. Fernlight looked in the mirror. Was she too generic? Like any sprite, she looked healthy and that wouldn't cut it. There was nothing she could do about her face, not at this point, but she could change her clothes.

"Give me a minute." She opened the closet that was built into the cabinets at the back of the office. Shedding her jacket, Fernlight took another off the hanger. It was a black hoodie, and it was scruffy enough to make her look more down on her luck. In the pocket were charms to enhance the disguise. She activated one labeled "Stale and A Little Ill". The first bloom of the scent made her eyes water, and she heard Bramble gagging in the front office. Then it settled around her and reduced to a bearable level. Bearable but detectable by humans.

She zipped the jacket and pulled the hoodie over her hair.

"Should I smell?" Bramble asked as she joined him.

"I think this will cover both of us," she said.

AN HOUR LATER, Fernlight stood in the mouth of the fourth alley. So far no one had any information, even when asked outright about a magic drug. The only benefit from the night was Bramble getting more comfortable about speaking with humans. Even he could see that these were no danger to a Real Folk. They were pitiful, both the users and the dealers.

"Can we go home after this?" Bramble whispered. "I don't think I can take anymore. It's sad. And I need rest, and we could be talking to Heath."

Fernlight drooped with fatigue too. It was like the atmosphere was sucking her spirit out and leaving her empty. If they couldn't do more than an hour investigating, they would never be successful. Next time they would be better prepared.

"We've covered half the area," she reminded Bramble. "But we should probably regroup and come back later."

"Tomorrow?"

"Later tonight. We can't waste time."

Bramble sighed, but didn't argue.

Fernlight glanced into the alley again. Four humans clustered around a small fire. She could feel the desperation from where she stood. "We go in. We ask our questions, and we leave."

"I'll go first," Bramble said. "I just don't think I can ask the questions."

Bramble fit in more. The last group had even asked if he was tweaking. They thought he was a human seeking drugs.

"Fine. Just remember everything they say. We'll need to make a report."

Bramble shuffled into the center of the alley, Fernlight lurked behind him. This was the most successful combination of behavior they'd found.

"Get lost," the closest human said.

"Just looking for some warmth," Fernlight mumbled.

Before any of the humans could react, Fernlight and Bramble were part of their circle.

"We don't have any fucking drugs," a second human said. This one was thin and shaky. "None to share."

"Don' say that," the third human hissed. This one was a woman, although all of them were sexless at first glance.

"We don't want to take your stuff," Fernlight said. "We aren't looking for the usual anyway."

That seemed to get their attention.

"Can you pay?" the woman asked. "If we gonna get you something special, it's gonna cost."

Hope kindled in Fernlight's heart. "We can pay."

"Show us." This was from the fourth human. Looking a little more well fed, perhaps a dealer.

"No," Bramble said. "Don't need you to know what we got. Don't know you."

"What can you get us?" This conversation was the most fruitful so far.

"Fenta? Crack? Rollers? Blinders?" The woman said.

Fernlight knew they were drugs, but not specifically what each did. But they were current street drugs and wouldn't be what they were looking for.

"More special than that," Fernlight said. If only she could just come out and ask about a magic drug.

The fourth human stepped a little close, and Fernlight saw he was a teenager, face freckled and ravaged by acne. "You need to talk to someone I know," he said, his breath rancid.

Bramble tugged on her sleeve. "Look," he pointed to the other end of the alley. Someone human, or humanlike, stood there.

Tall and well-muscled, he exuded threat. His physical intimidation was not why Bramble pointed. Around him, faint but visible to both Real Folk, was a blue glow.

Chapter 8

The figure darted to the right and disappeared on the street.

Fernlight led Bramble in a rush to get to the end of the alley, hoping the figure would still be visible when they got there.

"Hey, where you going?" One of the men around the fire called after them.

She turned to the right and came to a full stop. No one was in sight, glowing or otherwise.

"Now what?" Bramble asked. "That was him. I know it. He was the man in the spell, or the man who made the drug. How are we going to catch him?"

Fernlight looked at Bramble. "You are floating."

"Oops," he said and drifted back to the street.

The only thing she could think of was to use a tracking spell. "I'll make the spell as simple as possible. Let's hope the glow fades fast."

"I'll keep lookout." Bramble looked around and then floated to a window ledge two floors above them.

Fernlight needed power to give the spell, she couldn't afford to use any of her own or the glow of magic would give her away for hours. Even in the seediest part of the city, in the darkest corners, some convolvulus grew. Here, it sprouted from a crack in the building.

Fernlight gently touched the dusty green leaves. "Lend me your power, please. Only a little."

As a sprite, she could simply have taken the magic, but also as a sprite, she would never violate a plant in that way.

She felt a trickle of power on her fingertips and pulled away as soon as she had enough. "Thank you."

Fernlight switched on her sprite vision. Everything faded into gray and brown. Everything except three footprints that shone blue. As she bent to cast her spell, one of them faded away. Magic for certain.

She spoke the words of the tracking spell over a handful of the grit from the gutter, then tossed it in the air. The grit formed a long string and then started to snake its way forward. They could follow it until they found the target.

Fernlight waved to Bramble who flew down to join her, the glamor setting over him again as his feet touched the pavement.

There was no need to run, they would find him eventually, but while the streets were deserted, Fernlight wanted speed.

Two blocks down, their path ended at Hastings Street. The spell drew them on, but the crowded sidewalks slowed them to a walk. Too many police cars on the street. Fernlight couldn't risk attracting attention by running.

"What are we going to do when we find him?" Bramble asked as they twisted and stepped around a group of drug dealers.

"I haven't thought that far in advance," Fernlight admitted. "I guess it will depend on what we find."

"We need to know who it is before we tell Mamoru," Bramble said. "We might be finished, right? This might be the creator. It's not the person in the vision, too bulky. That man was skinny. Well, skinny when he was screaming. But even when he wasn't he was thinner than this guy. Did you find out if this is a human? Did you add that to the tracking spell?"

"Bramble, slow down. I didn't want to use the magic needed to do more than track him. Remember, we're supposed to keep magic to a minimum."

"So? What will we do?"

Fernlight stared ahead at the tracking spell. The dirt she'd charmed was plastered against the door of one of the new condominiums springing up on the edge of the area. Their luck held. It wasn't on a lobby door. It was on the front door to a unit. As soon as they stepped close enough, the grit slid to the ground. Whoever this blue person was, they were inside.

"What now?" Bramble asked. He looked around the area. "There's no good place to hide."

Doorways lined up for half the block, each one with a small recess under a tiny roof. Each one with a bright porch light keeping the area free of riffraff. Fernlight couldn't blame them; when you intrude your life into a shadowy world, you need to be careful. "We have to move away," she said. "I'll go up on the roof of that building." She pointed across the street to an old warehouse. The brick facade would give her plenty of handholds for the climb. "You watch from here until I'm up, then join me."

"I can get there faster," Bramble said. "Too bad I can't carry you. You watch for a minute while I go. I'll whistle when I'm set, and then you can climb, and I can watch and if he comes out, I will see him."

Fernlight nodded and tried to look as inconspicuous as a six-foot sprite could while Bramble flew. It was only a few seconds before he whistled. She ran across the street and searched for a way to the back, or the side of the building where she would be less likely to be seen. There were none, so she rushed to the roof, grabbing window ledges to heft herself up. Then she stood in the shadow of the stair access door and watched the building across the street.

"If we could use magic, we could see inside," Bramble whispered. "If Mamoru won't let us use it, why did he hire a magical detective agency? I've been wondering about that. And should I report that we used a tracking spell? Do you think he'd call that magic? I know it is, but it's not like a big spell..."

Fernlight let Bramble chatter on, knowing he didn't really want an answer. Bramble thought out loud, and sometimes it helped to hear him.

BRAMBLE KNEW Fernlight wasn't listening, but it didn't matter. It passed the time to talk, and it helped him to think about the case. His voice was getting tired now. He didn't know how long they'd been watching, but it was a long time. Fernlight usually told him about time and stuff.

"Shh," she said, touching his arm.

He didn't need to ask why; the door was open across the street. It was time for action.

"Are we going to follow him?" Bramble asked, flexing his wings to get them ready to carry him to the street.

Fernlight was leaning forward. What did she see? Bramble scrambled to the edge of the roof and leaned out. The man looked the same. Bramble blinked. No! He wasn't blue! "His magic glow faded too quickly. Maybe he knows how to do that for everyone. That would be great, to be able to do magic without everyone knowing. That would make our business successful. We could just use locator spells and truth spells to solve cases." He looked back to Fernlight, who was searching the street.

"We need to see what's in his house." She stepped on the ledge and then off it to land on a window ledge below.

As Bramble watched, Fernlight hopped from one window

ledge to the other then landed on the street. He flitted to join her. "Too bad you can't go up the same way. You were almost as fast as me coming down."

"It's hard to jump up," she said. "Fly over his house and see if you can find a way inside."

She melted into the shadows of the doorway. It wouldn't hide her from close scrutiny, but it would do. Bramble touched the camouflage charm in his pocket. *No magic!*

He flew to a window on the second floor. It was locked and he couldn't spend time here trying to unlock it. There was a window on the ground floor. The blinds were down, but maybe a fairy could peek through the holes in the slats. It would be something Fernlight couldn't do and that made him feel important.

He hovered close to the window and saw that the blinds weren't fully closed. He could see across the room, probably a human wouldn't be able to because there were no lights, so the man felt secure against someone breaking in to take his stuff. Across the room, Bramble could see into the back room. It was a kitchen, and there was a door that would lead to the outside.

Bramble flew over the roof of the unit and saw that the back was a big garden. It was pretty and they probably had some lily fairies and some pansy ones because the flowers were healthy and big. Why no one wanted Brambles in their yard was a mystery, but that's why he partnered with Fernlight. The garden was really secure. One door to each unit and one to somewhere else. Maybe parking? All of the windows facing the garden were dark.

He placed his hand on the lock and sent a probe of magic through the mechanism. It was like the tracker spell, not really magic, but maybe it was a good idea to keep this secret. Mamoru might not be happy if they went in without an invitation. But they had to find out what was inside.

The lock clicked and Bramble tried the handle. It opened

and something started beeping. An alarm! Bramble flew around the kitchen in a panic. Where was the keypad? How long did he have? A panel on the wall beside the door shone with a pale light. Bramble pressed his hand against it and sent magic into the circuits. "Shush. It's okay. We are friends." He knew the words weren't needed, but he had to do something to calm himself. He should have told Fernlight what he was doing. She might have thought about the alarm and then he wouldn't have been surprised.

One last beep and then the magic overwhelmed the circuits. The man would think there was some power surge. It was good that Real Folk didn't covet human things. Well, the sidhe did, but they wouldn't go to the trouble of breaking in. All the security was for protection against humans.

He flitted to the front door and twisted the deadbolt. He opened the door and beckoned to Fernlight. She checked the street before running to join him. There were a few people outside, but they didn't notice anything was wrong. Then he realized that maybe they did but refused to get involved. Humans were odd.

When they were standing in the living room, door closed, Bramble said, "Where do we start? Do we stay together? How long do you think we have?"

"Let's start upstairs," Fernlight said as she stalked to the staircase.

Bramble followed her. "Should we have gloves? Do we leave fingerprints? Will they know we've been here?"

"I don't think they make gloves in fairy size. We'll have to wipe things we touch and hope no one checks." She opened the first door. A bathroom.

It was a small room; Fernlight almost filled it. Bramble squeezed around her and found himself facing a counter that was covered in little pots and tubes. "This is interesting. It looks like stuff to make a disguise."

Fernlight pulled his hand away before he could touch the closest tube. "Try to read what it says first. I don't want to have to wipe everything in here."

Bramble shrugged. "Foundation, concealer, toothpaste, whitener. What are these?"

Fernlight was looking at a small pot trying to read the label on the back by leaning over it. "Make-up," she said. "Those are all things that humans use to make them look better. Read this for me, please."

Bramble wanted to touch the pretty powders that contained sparkling eyeshadow, he would look pretty with that on his face. His wife would like it too. Could they just take a little?

"Bramble," Fernlight said. It was in that tone that told him she'd already asked him something when he was busy with the pretty powder. Oh, yes, she had, but now he forgot what.

"What?"

"Can you read this without moving the jar?"

He craned his neck to look at most of the words. "Not all of it. It says, *apply sparingly, do not use in direct sunlight. Effect wears off...* I can't see the rest."

Fernlight looked around and then took a small towel off the rack behind him crowding his wings in the process.

Using the towel, she picked up the jar, and finished reading. "*Effect wears off in two hours, to remove sooner, wipe with rubbing alcohol.* It's called Sidhe Glow."

She twisted the cap off and looked inside and turned the jar toward him.

"It's make-up?" Bramble asked. "That's all the blue glow was?"

"Yes," she said. "We've wasted all this time."

Chapter 9

A door slammed and lights came on. Someone swore and Fernlight heard what could only be a fist hitting the wall.

"Don't panic," she whispered to the already trembling Bramble. "We have to hide until we can sneak out."

"Where?" Bramble's voice was barely above a breath.

Fernlight looked out of the bathroom. "He's still downstairs; we can hide in the next room." She placed the pot of fake magic glow on the countertop and pulled Bramble with her. The next room turned out to be a bedroom that was used for storage. Maybe their luck would hold and the man wouldn't come in looking for something from one of the boxes.

As soon as she released him, Bramble flew behind a stack of boxes. It was tall enough to hide her, but too tall for Fernlight to climb over without bashing into the ceiling. She carefully shifted it to make a space. Bramble was still glowing from the spells he'd used to break in. Fernlight shucked her jacket and used it to cover him.

"Why did he swear?" Bramble asked.

"I heard exactly what you did," she said then held up her hand.

The man was stamping his way up to them, talking loudly.

"Yeah, Keenan Jones. The alarm is burned out again," he said. "This is the second fucking time this month. I want a new one installed, and I want it first thing tomorrow."

"No," he said after a pause, "I don't care about your policy. The freaking thing is defective, and I need security."

He must have cowed the person on the other end of the call because he ended it with "yeah, six is fine. Don't be late."

Fernlight looked down at Bramble who was hiding under the jacket. When she raised an eyebrow, he simply pasted an innocent look on his face then looked away.

"Did you have to break it? We were lucky he didn't assume someone was here."

Bramble didn't answer. Fernlight could feel the vibrations of his trembling in the small space. She knew how much control he was exerting not to burst out of their hiding place and run for the door.

"As soon as it's safe," she whispered. "I won't let him hurt you."

Bramble blinked. "I won't let him hurt you either, partner."

Fernlight noticed that Bramble no longer glowed. Fear must be another way to clear the after-effects of magic. Why would a human want to glow like that? Real Folk went to huge lengths to avoid walking in the world with the mark of power. It felt rude. At least to Fernlight and her friends. A blazing reminder that they were different.

"It's quiet now," Bramble said. "Maybe we could try to leave?"

"He didn't go back down," she said. "I think he's in the other room, the other bedroom is my guess." Fernlight hoped the man snored. If he fell asleep they would move, but only when they knew for sure.

Across the hall, a drawer slammed, and heavy footsteps approached them. Bramble stopped breathing. Then let out a lungful when another door slammed. The man was in the bathroom, with the door closed.

Fernlight eased herself out from behind the stack of boxes, holding up a hand to make Bramble stay put. Just because the man, Keenan, was in the bathroom, it didn't mean he was staying there long enough for them to escape.

She made it to the door without tripping or knocking over a box. Turning the handle, she opened the door just enough to see what was going on.

The other bedroom faced her, and it was almost the same mess as Heath's home. Clothes, mostly black, were strewn across the bed, and over the floor. A jacket hung from the shade of a bedside lamp. The lamp gave off a blue-tinged light.

She almost leapt into the hall when she felt something touch her leg. Bramble. He was still trembling, but now he was directly behind her.

"I think he's going out again," Fernlight said. "The clothes he was wearing when we saw him first are in a pile on the floor."

"Maybe he's going to bed?" Bramble asked.

"Maybe, but we'll have to wait."

He blinked at her then mouthed "Okay."

"We'll listen," she said. "We can always hide if he comes this way, but it's better if we know what's going on."

Bramble didn't answer, his focus was on the hall.

Fernlight heard drawers open and close in the bathroom. A few muttered sounds came through, but not clearly enough for them to make out the words.

Then, just as she was thinking of sneaking down the stairs, the bathroom door swung open. Keenan stamped back to the bedroom, swearing under his breath with every step.

Had they disturbed anything? Did he know they were there, in his house somewhere? The only real information the sight of Keenan brought was confirmation that he was not going to bed. He wore a shiny blue jacket over dark jeans, and he smelled of something floral.

"Where the fuck are you?" he shouted as he came back into the hall. Luckily, he didn't look up, but turned to the stairs, stomping to the bottom.

"Is he talking to someone?" Bramble asked, his abject terror fading to just fear as he peeked around Fernlight's legs.

"I think he talks to himself," she answered.

"Great," Keenan said. Starting up the stairs again.

Fernlight pushed Bramble back into their room and held the door closed, with a crack only big enough for her to see if Keenan started toward them.

He was looking at a mobile phone when he came into view. A different one from earlier. This was plain and small, he held it close as he stabbed at the screen. Then he held it to his ear as he went back into the bathroom.

"It's me," he said.

Fernlight pressed her ear against the crack in the door. Keenan's voice was muffled, but she could make out the words as long as there were no other distractions. She turned and asked Bramble to keep quiet.

"It's not good enough," Keenan said.

A click of something being dropped onto the counter.

"It fades too fast, and it doesn't look real." He swore again. "No. I told them I wouldn't give it out. I don't care what they threaten to do. I keep my word."

He sighed as he listened. "No. I don't think they will act on it. There's no money in it. And I promised to keep the real shit a secret."

A pause.

"Yeah, it fools some people. But I need to look like one of them for longer than a couple of hours. This guy you said was testing it — the real shit — what's his angle?"

A drawer opened and closed.

"Fine, I guess I don't need to know. Just once the event is over, I need some to distribute."

Fernlight heard a click.

"I know it won't look right to one of the magicals. It's for the junkies."

Pause.

"Yeah, if you want this to work, they need to think it will make them magic. Yeah. When is it going to be ready? I can only keep up the interest so long before they start looking for a real drug. Your clients wouldn't like that."

Another click on the counter.

"How the fuck much?"

Something hit the floor and skittered across the tiles.

"I don't care. It needs to be cheaper. I don't care what you think, we don't make our money on rich fucks who are bored. We need it to be cheap enough for junkies. There are more of them."

A longer pause.

"I need some so I can get a taste."

Keenan sighed. "I know. This is different. It's not addictive right away. You said that!"

Another pause, and then, "Yeah, I'll go hang out at the right clubs. I'll make sure the marks are ready."

A long pause and then, "I said I would. Go back to making it and leave the distribution to me."

The conversation ended. Fernlight stayed motionless as Keenan left the bathroom. The man looked very different. His eyes were ringed in iridescent purple; a fresh blue aura shone from his pale skin. A gold ring hung from his reddened lip and five others from the earlobe she could see.

She held her breath, willing him to leave.

Keenan turned back to the mess of his bedroom and took a white scarf from the back of the door. He wrapped it loosely around his neck and smoothed his hair at the sides. Then, much calmer, turned to descend the stairs.

Fernlight breathed out and eased the door a little wider.

"Fucking alarm." Keenan slammed the door behind him.

Fernlight stepped into the hall and across to the bathroom. If the phone was still there, Bramble might be able to find out who Keenan called.

A siren wailed closer. Then another.

"They know we're here!" Bramble shrieked. "We have to go now!" He rushed past her and flew down the stairs.

The sirens passed.

Inside the bathroom, the counters were marked with colored dust patches. The pot of blue cream was gone. A phone sat in a smear of the white powder that he used on his face.

Fernlight reached for the phone. A voice inside said she should leave it. That he'd come home and find it missing. But a louder voice said, she could return it. That the information it might contain was too valuable to leave. If Bramble didn't know how to trace the call, Mamoru surely would.

"Fernlight, come on." Bramble's voice was strained. It was heartening to know he wouldn't run away and leave her here; it was frustrating that he was right. They couldn't linger. She slid the phone into her pocket and wiped a blue smear from the counter with a tissue. Mamoru would know what to do with the sample of the cream; or taking it to Heath might be better first.

This time they left by the front door, after checking the street through the window. No need to worry that they'd be seen, this neighborhood seemed to take on a mind-your-own-business attitude.

"Where to?" Bramble asked. His barely controlled panic had calmed to a more usual level of anxiety. "We could follow him again, or we could go to see Heath, or we could call

Mamoru, but it's late and we can tell him tomorrow what we found, unless you think it's so important that we need to call him."

They were halfway back to the original alley before his voice dropped off. Fernlight was glad they didn't have to be as careful on the way back.

"Home." Fernlight turned the corner; their friends from earlier were gone. The alley was deserted. "Don't you have to visit your family?"

"Not if we are on a case," Bramble said. "I can be away for up to two whole days before anyone will worry."

Two days was a long time for a fairy. Fernlight was glad to be independent. Unless Beacon called for her, and she kept a luck charm that he didn't, she could stay away as long as she wanted. It was only when she returned to the forest, what the humans called Stanley Park, that she had to do her sprite duty; enrich the ground and heal any plants that were in need.

"I think we go back to the office," she said. "We need to decide what to tell Mamoru, and what to ask Heath to do." She touched the pocket containing the phone and sample of the cream. "I don't think we can keep doing this without real magic. We have to figure out how to convince Mamoru to be okay with it."

"What if we can't?" Bramble hurried past her to open the door to the office. "And what about finding out who he was talking to? And these mysterious people who are threatening him. And maybe the alarm wasn't broken before. Maybe a wizard visited him, or a human with a spell to disable it."

Fernlight had been worrying over the same questions. "There are a lot of complications. Do you think it's a good idea to walk away?"

"From this? Or the case? It would be bad for us to tell our first client that we quit. It would be bad to let this go. HOP-D can't solve this. We have to continue anyway. We don't need the money — well, we need enough to buy honey, but that's not much. And maybe it always is that way. Maybe all kinds of clues come and then you have to decide what is real."

"It will be dangerous to continue without Mamoru's support." She opened the secret cupboard in the back of the file cabinets. Releasing the spell that kept everything inside safe, she deposited their evidence and reset the spell.

"You want to quit?" Bramble's voice squeaked with disbelief.

"I didn't say that."

"We should call Mamoru now," Bramble said reaching for the phone. "We need to know."

Fernlight held the phone down. "Not right away. I want to be very sure he's not part of the problem."

"You mean he is the source of the drug?" Bramble stepped back, his mouth open in surprise.

Fernlight didn't know anything for sure, and that was the problem. "Most potions use plants in their ingredients. Plants are powerful and contain the deep magic of the earth they grow in. So, whatever the drug is, there's a plant involved. I'm going into the forest and asking some questions. You go home. It might be much longer than two days before you get another chance."

Chapter 10

The night with his family was fun. Bramble felt refreshed and hopeful. Well, also worried and panicky. Why did Fernlight think their client was not honest? What had she found out overnight? How could they stop this drug from spreading through the humans? What would happen when humans could do magic?

He sighed out the tension as he opened the door to the office. A nice saucer of honey would help him get back to the happy feelings.

Fernlight was sitting on the floor with her back against his desk. She was asleep.

Bramble floated a little off the floor. He didn't want to wake her because, maybe, she would stop him getting his honey. And when she woke up, all the bad things could come true. So, just a little longer would be better.

"Good night?" she asked, opening her eyes.

"Sorry I woke you. Yes, it was a good night. Did you learn anything in the forest?" He floated closer to where the honey was stored.

"More about what's not happening than any real clues."

She stretched and rose to reach past Bramble and open the honey jar for him. "HOP-D isn't poking around. No one knows of any odd requests for any plant. No one knows anything about a drug."

Bramble slurped honey directly from the spoon. "Okay, what's next?"

"You need to report to Mamoru and tell him we will start using magic."

She was so abrupt all the time, Bramble thought, could he practice that? "It would be better to convince him instead. Humans don't like to be told what to do."

"It will take too long," Fernlight said. "I was wrong to delay the call. I'm more worried than before."

"Because no one had heard anything? I would be surprised if they did. Forest folk don't come out here. How would they learn about this? The best people to talk to would be the fairies because they see humans all the time. Although I don't know how they can handle it, being near them so often. Or a wizard, but we already did that. Or maybe Queen Maeve? The sidhe talk to the humans just like they are Real Folk."

"Maeve is busy. I asked for an audience last night. I got an appointment in two weeks." Fernlight tapped Mamoru's business card on the desktop. "I don't think we have two weeks."

Bramble licked the last of the honey from the spoon and placed it on the desk. "I will call Mamoru. I will convince him to let us do magic."

"And if he won't?"

He looked deep into her eyes. Something was wrong. Fernlight was the smart one and she was acting like there was no hope. "If he won't we can lie to him about how we solved the case."

"Lying to the client? Isn't that like quitting?" She smiled as she said the words.

Good, she is getting her humor back. "He won't know we're lying if we are careful. He'll definitely know we quit. You see, lying is better?"

That made her laugh. He didn't know why. It wasn't funny.

He reached for the phone and Fernlight didn't do anything, so he dialed the numbers.

"Please, call us back." He ended the call.

"What was that?" Fernlight asked.

"His voicemail. I didn't want to waste time."

That time she laughed real loud and long.

"What do we do while we wait?" Bramble asked.

Before Fernlight answered the phone rang.

"The Magic Search Ag— Oh, hello, Mamoru." Bramble tapped the picture that would put the phone on speaker.

"You have a report?" He sounded rushed. All humans always sounded rushed to Bramble, but this time Mamoru sounded more rushed.

"We have two pieces of evidence that we can give you," Bramble said. "And some proof that the drug is real."

"What kind of proof?"

Bramble sorted out the memories so that he could tell it like a human, not like a fairy. Humans were bad at picking out the important parts of a conversation. Next time Bramble would rehearse.

"First, we followed a human who glowed like he had performed magic. Then we were in his house and heard him talking to someone about getting the drug. We think he is going to sell it. Then we left."

"You broke into his house?"

The way he said it gave Bramble pause. How else would they get evidence? "I only broke the alarm. We have an example of some cream he is using that makes him glow like he did magic. And we have his phone which you might be able to use to find out who he called."

"HOP-D is held to the same standards as the police when it

comes to obtaining evidence." Mamoru paused for a moment. Bramble didn't speak because he didn't know what that meant. "I can find someone to analyze the calls," he continued. "We'll just have to find another way to explain how we got the information. Maybe I can get a tech to look at the cream, but it seems like something that a teenager would use to pretend they were magical folk."

Fernlight nudged Bramble and he glared at her. He hadn't forgotten.

"Can I ask a question," Bramble asked in his sweetest voice.

"Yes," Mamoru said.

"You asked us to not use magic, but you hired us, and we are a magical agency. And we are both full of magic and this drug is magic. Why can't we use magic?"

"I don't want something to go wrong. If we solve this, a good lawyer will say you used magic to force their client to do things."

"But we wouldn't!" Fernlight blurted out.

Bramble couldn't blame her, but it didn't help him convince Mamoru. And she kind of got him off his rhythm. He glared at her and held his finger to his lips.

"It's not about what you would do," Mamoru said. "It's about what they can accuse you of doing."

"Yes, I understand," Bramble said. "But if you could find this drug and the people involved without magic, then you would have."

"Is there some way to prove you didn't coerce someone?"

And that was the big question that kept humans and Real Folk apart. "None that humans would trust. Can you prove you didn't coerce someone?" He tried to make the last part sound like an innocent question, but there was accusation in there.

"Yes, usually," Mamoru said. "What kind of magic would you use?"

He was halfway there. "Tracking spells, maybe a truth spell, maybe a restraint spell. Kind of like handcuffs and a lie detector, but better." Don't keep talking.

"Is that all?"

"It will depend on the circumstances," Bramble said. Then held his breath. He knew Mamoru wanted to say yes. Fernlight's suspicions were unfounded, Bramble was sure.

"Do not use the truth spell on the perpetrator until a human is present."

"Thank you," Bramble said, and then ended the call before Mamoru could add more restrictions.

"You did well," Fernlight said. "But you didn't arrange to give him the phone and cream."

Bramble grinned. He was very smart and sneaky. "If it was that important, he would have asked. And maybe Heath should look at them first."

Chapter 11

Heath turned over the phone in his hands. "It's going to take a while." He put it on the desk and reached for the smear of blue cream.

"Be careful to leave enough for us to give a sample to Mamoru," Fernlight said.

Heath was in their office this time. Fernlight liked the space and it was neat. He'd brought a large canvas bag and she'd watched as he unpacked envelopes of herbs, seeds, and powders. Then he'd pulled out a box of the salted strings, a small copper pot, and some kindling.

"Can I have half?" He took the tissue in both hands. "That way I won't contaminate the other portion. We don't want HOP-D thinking I'm the criminal."

"They already think that because you are a wizard," Bramble said.

"Take half." Fernlight dug out a pair of scissors from her desk drawer. "How long with the phone?"

"Probably a few hours; the electronics inside make it complicated to find the paths to follow." Heath took one of the strings and glanced around measuring the space. "We'll set the circle here. Can you push the desks back and give me a bit more room?"

Bramble tried to push a desk and it wouldn't move. He looked at Fernlight; his plea for help didn't need words. He wheeled the chairs to the back to make room.

"Will the phone survive?" Fernlight asked as she pushed the desk. It wasn't heavy, but height gave her more leverage than Bramble.

"Probably," Heath said. "Is that important?"

"Mamoru knows we have it, and we might have to put it back." Fernlight placed three cushions into the center of the room. If they were going to be casting all day, she wanted to be comfortable.

Heath took a second string from his supply. "Get in the center. I warded the corners when I came in to discourage people from trying to enter. I'm going to double the circle so we don't risk running out of protection in the middle of the search. It should act the same as the general wards on my home."

She hadn't noticed him casting protections. "Was the ward something you got from your partners?" She was still bothered that Heath refused to tell her anything about them. For all she knew, they could be behind the drugs. Every time she tried to find out more, Heath deflected the questions.

"No, that's one of mine," Heath said without looking up. "Are you going to join me?" He nodded to the space in front of him.

Fernlight sat to the right of Bramble. Heath tossed the first string in a wide circle then laid the other alongside, making sure there was a connection at the four cardinal points. This was the first time Fernlight had seen a wizard power one circle from another. Without the string, it probably took more power than it was worth. Maybe there was room for efficiencies in magic.

Heath said the words to ignite the spell. Fernlight's ears popped at the sudden change of pressure. Bramble squeaked and rose from the cushion, wings flickering.

"Sorry, I should have warned you," Heath said. His voice was flat. The double circle was muffling him. "It will pass. Try holding your nose and then blowing out of it."

Fernlight followed the instructions and her ears popped again.

Bramble simply shook his head like a rattle and then smiled. "That's better." He floated back to the cushion.

Heath placed the phone and the smeared tissue on the floor between them. "I think we should start with the simple stuff first. Let's see what magic exists in this cream."

Fernlight watched as Heath muttered words over the tissue and flicked a few drops of oil off his fingers on the smear. "Hmm. No magic here. Look." He moved his hand out of the way and Fernlight saw tiny azure fish swimming above little indigo beetles and a pool of oil.

"The color comes mostly from the beetles; they crush them to make the dye. The fish give a bit of color, but mostly it's the bioluminescence. The oil is just a base product. Someone did a good job, but no magic." Heath looked at them and when neither Fernlight nor Bramble had questions, he waved his hand and the images disappeared.

"The phone?" Bramble asked. His eyes were shining; Fernlight knew he saw the technology as a toy.

Heath shook his head. "Later. Let's see if we can find out who this man was that we saw. Then it will be easier to see if he's connected to the phone. Unless you think the caller is more important than finding the user?"

Fernlight shook her head. "Let's keep going with our plan. If the answer is to be found in the phone records, it will take too long for us to find out."

Heath moved the phone and tissue behind his cushion and

reached for an envelope. When he ripped the seal open, Fernlight saw it was full of sesame seeds.

Heath poured them into a pile in the center. "Let's hope we don't get this many responses. I'm going to ask the spirit world to show us images of men who would want to have the power."

Fernlight swallowed a sudden fear. "This will show us how big the market for the drug is, right?"

Heath's eyes widened at her question. "Yes, and that will refine our search a little. Since we've been part of the human world, we've gotten much better at asking questions of the spirits."

"It's like searching the internet, right?" Bramble was staring at the pile of seeds. "The spirits don't care why we are asking. They just go looking for the information."

Heath chuckled. "Sort of. The difference is that the spirits are unpredictable. They might decide not to do the search, or that we've bothered them, or any number of reasons not to do the task. Getting the question right is a way to increase the probability of getting a usable answer."

He looked at Fernlight again. "You overheard this Keenan person say it's for rich people only, right?" Fernlight nodded and Heath continued. "We'll ask for people who would be able to afford it too. That way we get the real market not the market this Keenan fellow desires."

The difference went over Fernlight's head. "Whatever you think will work best."

Heath bent low over the pile of seeds. "Spirits of the circle. We wish information. For the one who finds an answer we offer beads of beautiful colors. For the one who finds the right answer, we have candy. We wish to know who in the human world would want to become a Real Folk, but only those with the means to purchase the method. Males only. Use the power in the seeds to assist you."

The seeds swirled immediately. Fernlight had seen these

kinds of summonings before. Not a modern technique, and it was good know that spirits still coveted small pretty things and sweet food. No one understood why. Spirits were not able to wear jewelry, nor eat the candy. But it worked, so everyone paid in beads and sweets.

Faces began appearing over the seeds. Two men, then three, then twenty, and then too many to count.

"Maybe we should have asked for local humans," Fernlight said.

"I did."

Chapter 12

Trying to reduce the number of images to a manageable amount was proving to be the hardest task. Fernlight's back ached and her legs were going numb. She shifted position in an attempt to bring some circulation to the sore areas; it only helped to shift the pain to different parts.

Bramble hovered above the ground, once again making her envious of his wings, but he wouldn't be able to maintain it much longer if the way he bobbed up and down was any indication. The only one who seemed unaffected was Heath. He barely moved as he asked question after question, tossing treats into the center with every answer, even if it was useless. How many could he have in his pockets?

"Fernlight?" Heath's word broke her concentration.

It sounded like he'd been asking something, but her mind was as worn out as her body. "What was the question?"

"We can do two more attempts before I run out of payment." Heath held out his hand showing two candies and a few beads. "We need a new approach. Or we have to stop and reset everything tomorrow."

She looked at Bramble who was deep in thought. His

hands twitching as though he was hitting the keyboard. "You are the search engine expert," she said, reaching out to touch him to get his attention.

"I'm thinking." Bramble didn't add anything more; a sure sign he was lost in a problem.

"We should wait for Bramble," Fernlight said. "How much longer will the circle hold?"

Heath shrugged. "Hours? Days? It's not the protection I'm worried about. It's that we are running out of questions."

They couldn't just throw away their last two chances to get answers now. "Give Bramble a few minutes. I can't even remember how we reduced the list to the fifty or so we have." However many answers, there were still too many to see enough detail to see their culprit.

"We've asked the spirits to eliminate those who are too old or too young. We all agreed that the man we saw was middle aged? Or just a bit less. Then we asked them to find out if any of them were too healthy to be taking a drug that did what we saw." He held up his hand as she started to protest. "It wasn't that simple. The first narrowing took two hours of subtle changes."

"I have an idea," Bramble said. "We think this is local only, right? I mean, the Keenan human was expecting to be given some of the drug, so it isn't likely to be someone on the other side of the world."

"We already established that these are all local people," Fernlight said a bit more impatiently than she meant.

"I know, but do we know that they are local right now?" Bramble asked.

"No," Heath said. "No, we assumed." He asked the question and tossed a bead and candy to the first spirit to respond. It took a few minutes — even the spirits were getting bored.

The number of images reduced by about ten. Now Fernlight could start to see details. As fewer images remained, they went from blurry sparks to tiny pictures.

"I wasn't finished," Bramble said. "We could have gotten two questions for that price. You need to wait until I finish!"

"Sorry," Heath said. "I thought you were done."

Seeing Heath humbled by her partner made Fernlight smile. Not at Heath's discomfort, but at the disparity of their sizes and demeanor. Even she sometimes forgot that Bramble was a full adult. Fairies were not what they seemed, and it was good to be reminded of that.

"I don't remember if we narrowed it down by looks. I know we didn't see much, and sometimes that means we forget that we might have seen something."

"You mean the flickering?" Fernlight asked. "Can we ask the spirits about someone who flickers?"

"Only if we knew what it meant," Heath said. "If we ask just about flickering, we might get people who are dozing off in a meeting. We need to know what he becomes when he's not human. If he's even human part of the time anymore."

Bramble floated between Fernlight and Heath. "That's a good idea, but it's not what I meant. I meant something more regular. Like we think we know how old he is, but maybe we were wrong with that, maybe we should ask the question not based on who we see now, but all the men who are local right now and whatever we agree on."

The thought of bringing back all of the images gave Fernlight a headache. "If we get too many, we'll have to look at each one." She shuddered at the time it would take.

"It's better than looking at a few that are all the wrong ones," Bramble said. "What do you remember? His eye color? The shape of his nose? The way his ears look? We will all remember a little bit of different information."

Fernlight stretched her arms over her head to get the

cramps and kinks out. "I remember he had short hair," she said. "But anyone can cut their hair."

Heath chuckled. "But no human can grow hair that fast. I remember he had a pointy chin, well kind of pointy."

"And he had small mouth," Bramble said. "Okay, that should be enough. Everyone get ready to remember what we see. We need to draw it for Mamoru when we leave the circle."

Heath took a deep breath and checked the pile of sesame seeds. Most of them were scorched from the spirits ripping the power from them. He brushed the worst aside, and made sure there was a clear patch of unburnt ones.

"Spirits who remain," he said. "We seek one who is a male human, who would have desire for magical power, who is currently in our area — within what the humans call the Metro Vancouver area. We also ask that you ignore previous questions and concentrate on this one only. Within the humans you find, we wish to see those with pointed chins, small mouths and short hair."

You have exhausted all but me. A voice echoed through the circle. *I demand all of the seeds and any other reward you carry.*

Heath looked at the other two. Bramble glared and then reached into his pocket drawing out a tiny vial. "Honey," he said.

Fernlight patted her pockets. The only thing she could find was the smear of blue cream. Since it wasn't the drug, no one needed to test it. "Would this interest you?"

She placed it on the floor and waited. A translucent claw poked through the tiles and hovered over the tissue.

It is different from the others. Spirits will envy me. I will take it.

"Not until you have performed." Heath tugged the tissue away.

A sigh blew through the circle. *Done.*

The seeds flared up, the tissue, honey vial and the remaining beads and candy all disappeared.

"One day we're going to figure out how they do that, and why," Heath said.

Then the circle filled with an image. The man in the vision.

He was talking to someone they couldn't see. He was reaching out his hand to take something. It was withheld until he passed a wad of money.

He held his prize in his hand. Looking at it like it was a lover. Then he began to twitch and started chewing his lip.

Fernlight watched in fascination as he attached the vial to a needle and jabbed it into his thigh. His eyes closed and he smiled, his face turning peaceful for a moment. The injection must have been to calm him, Fernlight thought.

She stared at him intently, cataloging his features and committing them to her memory.

"Can I end the spell?" Heath asked.

The man's eyes opened, and he turned to stare at Fernlight. "Not just yet," he said.

Chapter 13

He sees us! He sees me!

Bramble worked hard to stay conscious. His heart was going to escape through his mouth, his wings were flying on their own and he was rising to the top of the protection shield and that didn't feel like what a detective would do.

He blinked his eyes to stop them from closing and then thought at his wings and made them slow down. His heart followed his wings and then he felt the floor beneath his bum. *He sees me, but he can't get me.*

"How can a human do that? A live one I mean. Does he know who we are?" He pinched his lips between his fingers to stop them from asking stupid questions that no one could answer.

"Who are you?" The human asked. "Why are you watching me?"

The man was making him want to answer.

"What do you see, human?" Heath asked. His voice was different, it was commanding.

"Three beings," the man said. He leaned in close like he was trying to get a better look. "You must be magical. I am the only human with the ability to do magic, and I can't cast a circle yet."

YET! He was expecting to get stronger. Bramble swallowed.

"What is your name?" Heath asked.

"Why should I tell you?"

"I cast the circle; you are compelled to answer."

Bramble waited. It would be easier to solve the case if they knew who this man was. But, at least, they had a clear view of him. Bramble dug fairy sand from his pocket and sprinkled it on the ground. "Record him." The grains began crawling into a likeness of the man, colors changing to match his hair and eyes.

"I feel that," the man said. "But I don't see the hurry to obey. Tell me how you found me."

Bramble kept his ears on the conversation, but his eyes on the fairy sand. It should have stopped when it made the picture. It didn't. Almost half the grains were turning over constantly. This man was not just one man. How could that be?

"You wouldn't understand," Heath said. "It is only wizard magic. Others cast circles differently."

"That is interest…ing."

The gap in the word made Bramble look up. The human's face was twitching like the sand. One moment it was normal and then it became blue and there were cracks in the blue that seemed to lead to an abyss.

"Who are you? I expect an answer now." Heath slammed his hand on the tiles as he said the last word.

"I am one of a kind. For now. I am two…I am…two." He stopped speaking and squished his face up like he was trying to hold onto one of the sides of the flicker.

"Why are you doing that to yourself?" Fernlight asked. "It looks painful."

"Magic," the human gasped. "I will have magic when it is

done. And then I will come for you. I will stop this foolish attitude, and we will take our place as the rulers of the mundane. I just need a little more of the drug. When the change happens, I will not take any more. I must have more now."

That sounded like a lot of work. And why would the other Real Folk allow the wizards to run the world? And what would the druids do?

Bramble opened his mouth to say they didn't want to rule the world. Then he realized the human didn't mean fairies either. Would Heath want that?

"Help me make the transition," the man said.

"No. You must stop. We do not want to rule anyone," Heath said. "Stop trying to become one of us, it is not just magic that separates us from you humans."

"I will make the transition. There is no going back. I need more of it, I will get more of the drug." He leaned in even closer. It felt like he was trying to step through.

Bramble watched as the man started to flicker faster as he got more agitated. He said he could only see that three people were here. He couldn't tell who, which was a relief because the man was crazy, but even a crazy man might be able to find them. And maybe he would succeed. Then all he needed was to learn how to cast a circle and then he could summon them and then he'd know.

"I will succeed. Do not oppose me." He reached toward them and then flickered out of sight before he could finish moving.

"Is he gone?" Bramble asked.

Fernlight touched her ear and looked at him.

He dropped his voice a few octaves, even though sprites should be able to hear more than just that narrow band of sound. Maybe they could hear lower noises.

"I asked, is he gone?"

Heath blew out a long breath. "Yes. This is bad."

Fernlight stretched and Bramble knew that she was worried about what happened because she did that to give her time to think. He hoped that she had an idea because he didn't and... *stop panicking!*

"Do you have any idea why he's switching between states? Is it voluntary?" Fernlight asked.

Heath was clearing the remnants of the power from the circle and didn't answer right away. It made Bramble nervous to wait. And he almost interrupted Heath and then he remembered that if the circle wasn't cleared properly, they could release a spirit.

"I think the drug is changing him. I think the other side of his personality is where his future lies if we can't reverse it." He gathered the inner salt string. "This is going to take a lot of research."

"Why does he want to rule the world?" Bramble asked.

Heath released the outer salt string. "Humans aren't just non-magical," he said. "They think about the world differently. They breed indiscriminately and that means they run into shortages of things. Many of them want to take everything before someone can take it away from them."

"So, if he can rule the world, he gets to decide who can have food and space and stuff?" Bramble didn't understand why anyone would want that power. It was hard enough to lead his small tribe of fairies. How would he know what an imp needed? Or a nymph, or a sidhe? Maybe humans all wanted the same thing so the job of ruling would be easier. It would be way easier if the Real Folk were gone. *He wants to kill us.*

Then everything around him disappeared from his mind as he imagined how the humans would kill him.

Chapter 14

The office felt tainted with evil. Fernlight knew that there was no real leakage from the circle, but it didn't matter. They had locked up and moved to Heath's house. A place that might be cluttered, but it had a safe and homey atmosphere that helped to cleanse the stain of the meeting from her. Only once they were inside did she remember that the phone was still on the desk.

Bramble was still vibrating with anxiety. They needed to talk about what happened, but until he was calmed, the fairy wouldn't be able to add anything to the conversation.

"I'll get some honey," Heath said, leaving her with Bramble.

"See," Bramble squeaked. "I was right. The humans want to kill us. We need to stop them; we can't let this happen. Who was that man?" He took a breath to continue.

"Will you listen to me?" Fernlight asked. Sometimes letting him wind down by talking worked. This time she needed to speed up the process. He was half on the right track; this human needed to be stopped.

Heath returned with a saucer brimming with honey. "Eat this while we talk."

Fernlight smiled. Bramble was torn between his spiral of fear and the generous offer. While he decided, his wings slowed and his body stopped trembling. "Okay, convince me that we are safe." He took the saucer and perched on the edge of a chair; his eyes fixed on them while he dipped his finger in the honey.

Was this an improvement? Fernlight wasn't prepared for this reaction. She looked to Heath who shrugged. How did she know all humans were not at least hoping they would die out?

She cleared her throat. "He didn't say he would kill us," she said. "Why did you come to that conclusion?"

"No, he didn't say it, but it's what comes next. He will get magic. He will use us to help him take over the world, whether or not we do it willingly, and I think at least some of the sidhe would be willing because they think they will become the kings and queens, but then, when he's finished, there are only us, the Real Folk that might be able to stop him, and so he'll get rid of us."

So not just an emotional reaction. "You followed the logic well, but there are more options." She turned to Heath. "Have you researched human history?"

"Of course," Heath said. "You are thinking this man is not the first to want to take over the world. You are right."

Relieved that Heath seemed to follow her logic, Fernlight asked the next question. One that she hoped would trigger a new train of thought for Bramble. "So why are there so many rulers still."

"Humans are too independent and the world is too big," he said. "Kind of like why the sidhe haven't taken over the Real Folk."

Bramble sucked his finger clean of honey. "He seems very sure."

"If that was all it took to win the world, we'd be lost right now," Heath said.

Fernlight hoped the wizard was right because Bramble had put his sticky finger on the real problem. This man was very confident even though he didn't have the drug. They were drowning in their own uncertainties; they didn't know who he was, they didn't know who made the drug, what the drug actually did, and worse than all of that, they didn't know how to start finding the man.

"We have to get in his way," she said. "He may be confident because he knows a lot about how to control humans, but he doesn't know the Real Folk." If she didn't mention their limitations aloud, then perhaps she would sound as sure as their target. "Someone is behind this. Someone is making the drug."

Heath looked at her, waiting for more. When she didn't speak, he said, "It's not my partners. I know you suspect them, but I guarantee that they aren't behind it."

"How?" Bramble asked. "How can you guarantee it? How can you know any human is innocent?"

Heath shoved his hand into his pocket. "I tested them." He expression closed off any further questions.

"My picture!" Bramble yelled. He bounced off the chair, placing the empty saucer on the seat. "Will it still be there? I know it will help. That's why I did it. Maybe Heath can use it to find the man. Maybe I can find a way to put it in the internet so I can find his name. I shouldn't have left it when we came here. It was on the floor of the office."

Heath waved to get Bramble's attention.

The fairy ran out of words after a second or two. "Why are you doing that?"

"I have the picture here." Heath reached into his pocket and drew out a sheet of paper so thin it was see-through. "I transferred it to this substance when I released the wards."

He held up the sheet and the man from the circle looked back at Fernlight; she flinched. The face was recognizable, a perfect copy, but, on the edges, it dissolved into tiny dots of blue. Bramble's spell had tried to capture the transformation.

Bramble reached to touch the film holding the image together then held back before making contact. "Will it last when we try to show it around? Can we make copies? How long will the spell hold?"

"Slow down," Heath said. "Yes, it's stable. This spell should hold until we rip the film it's on."

Fernlight knew that Mamoru would need to see this image. "And the copies?"

"I'm afraid to try human methods," Heath said. "The process might destroy the image. We need someone to use magic to create the copy. Or, I guess, copies."

Bramble opened his jacket pocket wide. "I don't have enough fairy sand. I could try making the same spell and using the picture instead of the man. But it might not work because the picture is not alive."

And we don't have time. Fernlight tried to commit the picture to her memory, but she was so tense about the possibilities that it kept slipping out when she looked away. "Can we draw it?" she asked. "You can keep the original for your work, but Mamoru won't need anything more than a drawing. Bramble can find a way to get it into the internet from a drawing."

Bramble nodded, his body bouncing with enthusiasm. "I need paper and brushes, and lots of colors of ink."

"Can you draw?" Heath asked as he rose from his seat.

Bramble looked offended. "I'm a fairy; of course I can draw." He glanced at the film again. "It won't move like this does."

Chapter 15

"It's late," Fernlight reminded Bramble. They were back in the office; a lingering sense of wrongness was making her skin itch.

Bramble marched up to his desk and grabbed the phone. "Yes, but this is important. I'm sure he's available. If he wants us to solve the case he should be always available. And I'll tell him that if he doesn't answer." He pressed the keys on the phone as he spoke.

Fernlight waited until Bramble jerked into his business face. A fairy's idea of solemn; brows pulled together, a smile without showing teeth and a tip to his head like he was listening. *Another tip from the computer?*

"Yes, Mamoru," he said. Then he held out the phone from his ear. "Voicemail."

Fernlight reached for the phone, but Bramble simply kept talking.

"Mamoru. You need to be ready for our calls at all times. We do not know when an important piece of information will come into our hands. If we have to wait for you—"

Fernlight tried to wrest the phone from him, but Bramble flew out of her reach.

"We might miss our opportunity to stop this problem. If you are not there to advise us, we may have to use a lot of magic to save the day." He stopped speaking and held the phone out again. "It hung up on me!"

Fernlight reached for the phone again. "You probably used up all the time."

Bramble dodged her hand and dialed again.

"Just tell him we have a picture of the user and please call us," Fernlight blurted the words out.

"Mamoru, please call us as soon as humanly possible. We have a picture of the man who is using the drug." He ended the call. "What is the difference between humanly possible and just possible? I heard someone say that, and thought it sounded like a good way to say it's urgent, but now I think of it, I don't understand it."

Fernlight shook her head in answer. She took the drawing from Bramble and laid it flat on her desk. "How do you get this into the computer?"

"I will make a scan of it and then it will be there. We should give Mamoru a copy of the scanned picture and we should put this drawing in the safe." Bramble flitted over to one of the pieces of equipment and turned it on.

Fernlight watched as he placed the picture face down on the glass plate and pressed a button. Light moved from one end of the document to the other.

"Done," he said, lifting the picture from the glass. "Oh! Oh no!"

He turned the picture toward her and Fernlight saw the page was smeared. "But it didn't move," she said. "It looked right when you put it there."

"It is bad magic," Bramble said. "The man has control of his image. Let me check the computer, maybe it's fine. I wonder if Heath has noticed the same thing? If we can't share the picture with Mamoru, he will be very angry. But if he was there to take the call, maybe it wouldn't have happened. Or maybe it would have happened, but we would still have a copy."

Fernlight's head ached. One second they were almost done and the next they were back at the beginning. Was this what humans felt around magic? Like there was nothing stable? Bramble was right, Mamoru would lose confidence in them.

"It didn't work!" Bramble pointed to the screen.

Fernlight saw a smeared image on the screen. It was worse than the paper. "It looks like it was moving when the machine worked."

"I am going to write out what we saw," Bramble said, clicking the keyboard. "He had red hair and it was short. He had a pointy chin and a small mouth he was kind of skinny and he had green eyes and he kept cracking and it looked like there was a huge space beyond the cracks."

Fernlight nodded at each detail. "I don't think the cracking thing is happening in public," she said. "It would be obvious that there was something wrong. Humans don't do that."

Bramble saved the file and closed it. Then he opened it again. "It stayed. Maybe we fixed it. And maybe when Mamoru calls, I can draw it from memory so even if it doesn't last long, Mamoru will see what we saw."

Fernlight hoped Bramble was right. "We need to look for this man anyway."

"Yes, we should think about who would have this kind of money. Do you remember any of the other faces?"

"Not so much detail," Fernlight said. "Do you think searching for one of the others will lead us to our man?" It was a good idea. All of the images that filled the circle could afford the drug, and were the kind of human who would want power. And Keenan sounded sure that he could sell it, so there were more out there.

Bramble turned off the computer monitor. "I think we will

look at the internet to find rich men. If we see someone we recognize, it might be a lead."

"Why did you turn off the computer?" Fernlight was ready to stare at the screen all night if it would help.

"I am very tired. I need more fairy sand, and maybe a few other things, and I need to recharge my power and that means being with fairies. You should go to the forest and soak up some magic." Bramble gathered his discarded jacket and shoulder bag.

Now that she looked, Fernlight could see that Bramble was looking faded and fairies didn't have a way of storing their energy like sprites, and probably humans. "If I go to the forest, I take the risk that Beacon will assign me duties. I'll stay here. That way Mamoru will have someone to reach when he calls."

"Fine, I will be back before sunrise and then we start searching faces." He slipped through the door and took flight.

Fernlight locked the door behind him and moved to Bramble's seat. It was uncomfortably small, but if she was staying, then she might as well start searching. She wasn't as good as Bramble, but time and patience usually had their rewards.

She hit the switch on the side of the screen and waited. Nothing happened. She searched for another button, finding one on the side of the machine under Bramble's desk. Flipping it on resulted in a whirr of a fan and a slight spinning sound. The screen lit up with a picture of a bramble patch. In the center was a white box. That was where you typed a password. One that only Bramble knew.

Sighing, she moved to the floor and began a meditation on the wholeness of nature.

Chapter 16

"I know you want me to stay," Bramble said. His wife, Thorn, still didn't buy his plan to help the clan. "I have to be away again for a while. Maybe two days, maybe more. This is important. If we can solve this case it will mean we have a future. People, humans, will know that we are good. Then I can bring in Thistle and Briar. They will continue the work and then our tribe will be as important as the Rose Fairies." He stretched. It was fine to be taller out in the world. You needed height to be noticed. But here, at home, a few inches from the ground was perfect.

Thorn stood firmly on the ground, her arms crossed and that look on her face that told him he'd better stop talking.

"Two days is too long. You will be thin when you come back. It isn't healthy for you to be away from us." She looked up and around the hollow in their Bramble bush. "You are the King. You aren't here when we need you. You are off chasing a dream. Why do you want to be important? It is not our way."

Am I the only one who sees the future? "The humans don't like our type of flower. They aren't like Real Folk. They keep destroying our homes and we will die out. If we are important, we can stop that. We can keep bramble bushes in protected areas and thistles, and briars, and gorse. Everyone will be safe." He threw up his arms. "If I have to fade a bit to make that happen, then I'm happy to do it."

"You are exaggerating," Thorn said with a sigh. "We've been through this enough. I will not change my mind and you will not change yours. I suppose I will have to accept that or take another husband."

She won't be happy with anyone else. Bramble admitted that might be a lie. He was king, so Thorn was important in the tribe as his queen. Maybe she didn't think being important was a good thing. And he knew that she was right. His people needed him to solve the problems of being a weed fairy. That term hadn't existed five years ago. Humans invented it because they liked to pick what they liked and destroy what they didn't. Weed fairies were undesirable.

"I can't tell you what this is about," Bramble said. He couldn't quite convince himself that Thorn was someone who should know about the details and he wasn't going to break the oath. "But it makes our problems look insignificant. Fernlight and me, we think this case might be about saving the Real Folk and the humans."

"Take Briar with you," Thorn said. "You'll need help if this is so vital to our survival."

Bramble thought about how Fernlight might react. Then he realized it wasn't her reaction that he needed to worry about. He would be more focused on protecting his son than saving the world. "He will come on the next case. I need to make sure this is the right thing for the tribe before I bring in the kids. I promise I will teach him and Thistle next time."

Thorn sighed. "You can't tell me anything? I'm your wife."

Bramble felt the tug of the oath when she asked. "You will be too busy being the queen while I am away. You are much wiser than I am." She snorted at his attempt to flatter her.

Thorn always saw through his maneuvers. "No, I mean it. You make better decisions on the arguments people have. I am too busy thinking about how to save the tribe to worry about family tiffs."

He saw a smile tug her lips.

"Fine," she said. "If you can't tell me anything, I suppose we are stuck with the same situation. I need you to be healthy when you come back. How will we do that?"

Bramble also wanted to be healthy. "Maybe I can take a little of the treasure with me?" Carrying a few items soaked in fairy magic would work. Fairy treasure was kept close to the tribe and its location held tightly secret.

"I will not allow our king and our treasure to be in danger." Thorn turned to leave him standing alone. He knew it was a ploy, but it worked anyway.

"Stay. I can find another way," he pleaded. "I will use very little magic when I'm gone. That should help. I don't need the treasure. I thought we could visit for a few hours, but I can sleep on the hoard and that will give me a full charge."

"No. You will help me with the tribe's problems while you are here." She cleared a space on the ground of the fallen leaves. "I need your help with some of the bigger problems. There are rumors of a rogue wizard, as if that would have happened before."

Bramble wondered if anyone was trustworthy. Could a rogue wizard have created the drug? It didn't seem possible.

"It would help if you kept track of the destruction of our homes," Bramble said. He would find a way to charge his energy before going. Helping Thorn would get her closer to his side. He decided to take a risk and asked, "Would you take a secrecy oath?"

"I am your wife!"

He knew as soon as he asked that he should have explained first. "I think it would help you understand if I could tell you the details of our case. But I have promised not to tell anyone without an oath. It is not something I need, Thorn. It is the client."

She looked at him, suspicion painted over her face. "Let's look at these problems first. I will think on the oath."

Defeated, Bramble settled beside his wife and started sorting through the petitions for judgment.

Chapter 17

Bramble liked the city when it was quiet like this. The sun was not quite up, just casting a bit of light in the sky, like it was saying good morning. It reminded him of the stories of the days before. When humans didn't know about the Real Folk. He touched the two pretty gems in his pocket that Thorn had released from the treasury. The power in them slipped warmly through his fingertips.

The door to the office was closed and the blinds were drawn. Fernlight might be asleep so he should go in quietly. The closer he got to the office, the more he worried about telling Fernlight about his visit. Thorn had finally agreed to the oath. And when she heard about the case, she still didn't think it was necessary; she would have kept the secret without it. He would have to make that up to her.

He turned the key and slowly opened the door. He saw Fernlight sitting in front of the desks, eyes closed, a serene expression. Good. If she was calm, he wouldn't have to face another angry female. King or not, he had no idea how to stop getting in trouble with Thorn and he didn't want that to continue with Fernlight.

He floated just above the floor to avoid disturbing her and approached his chair. If she stayed in her trance, he would have time to do some more searching for the man.

"Did you have a nice visit?" Fernlight asked as Bramble sat.

"I didn't mean to interrupt," Bramble said, dodging the question.

"Are you fully charged?" She stood up and brought her chair beside his. "I would have done some work last night, but I don't know the password."

Bramble laughed. "Do you know how to search the vast universe that is the internet?"

She chuckled. "No, but you said I couldn't break it so I thought I'd try."

Bramble typed in his password, letting Fernlight see it. He would give her some training when they had time.

Having her sitting next to him was uncomfortable. Not because she was a threat, she would never hurt him. But because it reminded him that they had sworn not to keep important secrets. And telling Thorn about the case was the most important secret he had.

"Are you going to start the search?" Fernlight asked. "If I watch, I can learn. Will it take long?"

Bramble's throat itched with guilt. He coughed and it didn't all go away. He turned to Fernlight. "I have told Thorn about Mamoru, the drug, and HOP-D." He felt better already.

Fernlight drew back, alarm radiating from her. "We should have talked about that first."

He held up his hands. "I didn't plan on it. I wasn't going to tell her, but she made me. I needed her help to stay powered, she made me promise to keep it a secret how we do it, it's not an important secret, it is a fairy secret, so don't ask me. But telling her was the only way for me to get the power, and she agrees it's very dangerous, and that we need to stop it. And I made her take the oath even though she didn't want to." He ran out of breath.

"Okay," Fernlight said. "We should agree before we share the information in the future, but the oath will hold her. Now how do we find the name of this man?"

Bramble was all fired up for a fight and didn't know what to do with the defenses he had ready. "Okay? But why aren't you mad at me?"

Fernlight looked puzzled. "Why would I be mad? You used the oath, which, despite what we told Mamoru, you could have avoided with a little fairy logic, and it's in the past. Let's move forward."

It hadn't occurred to Bramble to circumvent the oath. It was more than a little fairy logic, and it would have hurt him a lot. He let it lie. "Yes. Well, it will take long probably, but maybe not. The internet holds lots of information, kind of like the spirit world. If you think of Google like an enormous spirit who wants to help, it might make it easier to understand." He started typing a search.

"You mean we have to know what to ask," Fernlight said. "Is Google the only spirit?"

Bramble looked at the list of possible leads from the search. "No, but it's the best to start with. Look, I searched for rich men in Vancouver. It's a very wide search so there are more than two million results." He leaned in to look at the screen. "Look, it includes people who have been in Vancouver, and it looks like there are other places called Vancouver. And some of these are not men."

"We don't have time to look at all of those," Fernlight said, leaning toward the screen. She saw the same headline on several results.

Bramble pushed her back so he could see. "We have to narrow it down. I will try to look at the first few results, and if we see anyone from the circle, we can search for people like him."

"How do we know what to choose?"

He knew Fernlight was trying to learn, but it was slowing him down. "You need to watch more and ask less. I don't know what it means to be like someone. I will know when I see it, and it might take a few hours. And when we have a narrower list, I might have to use other spirits."

"I'm in the way?"

Bramble really wanted to say yes and have her leave him alone. But he was her partner and if she knew more about his internet, maybe they would be more successful. "A bit. If you watch me for a while, and maybe write down your questions, I can answer them when we have time."

She took a pad of paper and a pen from her desk. "Ready."

For the next few hours they both read articles about rich men. There were similarities in the articles. Most of the men were members of clubs for golf, yachting, horse racing; some of them were members of something called the Terminal Club, which was a fancy businessman's place.

"What if we try something else." Fernlight was looking at her notes. "We've seen a lot of pictures of rich men, but the man we are looking for must not be famous, or must be very private."

"Yes," Bramble said. He rubbed his eyes and waited for her to continue.

"He must have a plan, right?"

Bramble nodded.

"If you were trying to take over the world, wouldn't you need to get your rivals together so you could control them?"

"You are thinking like a sidhe," Bramble said. "That's a good idea. So we should stop trying to find a picture of a man who doesn't like his picture taken, and look for an event or something that will give him an opportunity to get rid of his competition?" It was a weird way to think, but Bramble was sure they were on to something.

"Yes," Fernlight said. "How many events could there be?"

Bramble typed the search. "Four thousand."

"Better than two million," Fernlight said.

"Way better," Bramble said as he typed. "There will be a lot of duplications in the results. Some will be advertisements, some will be articles and news reports, some will be people talking about events." He narrowed his results and then sat back so they could both read the screen. "Ten events in Vancouver that will attract important people. I couldn't narrow it down to men, I guess humans don't have that kind of event, or at least don't advertise it, and maybe his competition is men and women." He was surprised his voice didn't shake as he started reading the details.

"If it's one of these events, we have five days. And we don't know where to start." Fernlight's voice did shake.

Chapter 18

Five days! Fernlight struggled to move beyond the fact that they had five days. It had been five days since Mamoru came to them. How were they going to find the man and whoever created the drug in five days?

"Maybe we didn't use the right logic," Bramble said, patting her arm.

The fact that he didn't ramble on broke her concentration on the impossibility of the task. "We have to believe it's right," she said.

"Then we need help," Bramble said. "Heath will be up now. Maybe he has some ideas or maybe he's found the man. And he has the original picture, maybe we can get it and show it to Mamoru."

If Heath had information, he would have called. Fernlight didn't know what else to do at this point, so she cast the small circle needed to contact Heath. She wanted to see him in the normal way, not on the phone.

"Good afternoon," Heath said as they connected. "And how are you this fine day?"

Hope bloomed for Fernlight; if Heath was this cheerful, he

must have something. "Not so well here," she said. "We are no further than we were."

"That's not true," Bramble said. "We think we have only five days to stop the man."

"That's not good news," Fernlight said.

"It's progress," Bramble said, frowning at her.

"I couldn't find the man, but I also got the clear message from the spirits that time is short." Heath reached behind him. "The picture is changing more now." He held up the sheet and Fernlight saw that there were patches of the man that remained blue. "I think it means he's getting closer to the full change."

The case was too full of 'I thinks' and empty of 'We knows'. Fernlight stared at the picture. The man was still recognizable. "We need to show this to Mamoru. Our copy is destroyed."

Heath blanched at her words. "I can bring it over," he said. "I don't want HOP-D in my house, not even one of the good ones." He laughed, but it sounded more scared than happy.

"We'll arrange it," Fernlight said. "Today. We will let you know when. Until then, keep that safe."

Heath nodded. "I have an idea."

The way he said it Fernlight knew he expected opposition. "We need to find the drug maker," Fernlight said.

"That's a good idea, and you can use a tracking spell, maybe. I'd try using cobalt and anything that is human, along with something that alternates between magic and mundane."

"Like what?" Bramble asked. "I don't know what that would be. Is there an herb, or is there a powder?"

Heath looked at Bramble and then glanced at his pocket. "There is something."

Bramble slid his hand into his pocket. "NO! It is not for that. I will not use fairy treasure for this. What if something goes wrong and he learns about fairy treasure and then steals it from us?"

Heath held up his hand in surrender. "It's up to you. I would use a newer piece that the magic hasn't—"

"Stop!" Bramble flitted toward Heath's image. "It is a fairy secret!"

Fernlight waited out the staring match between wizard and fairy. If Bramble's treasure would help, she'd get his cooperation. But he was right, it was a big risk. "We have another option." She realized that they had one piece of information. "We could follow Keenan."

Bramble broke his stare of domination with Heath. "Yes, and the spell to find him will not require fairy secrets. We have some of the cream he used. We know where he lives. We know he knows who can get the drug. Good idea, partner." The last was said with a glare at Heath.

"Okay, I leave it to you," Heath said. "Now do you want to hear my idea?"

Fernlight itched to start following Keenan, but she couldn't let Heath do what he wanted. Wizards sometimes followed the magic knowledge without thought to the consequences. It was unlikely that a wizard created the drug. Although there was no real way to understand how the prophecy had changed them.

"I can try to make a cure," Heath said. "Everything has a cure."

"How?" Bramble asked. "If you don't have the spell to create the drug, how will you make a cure? That sounds like a waste of time."

She knew there was lingering resentment from Heath's suggestion earlier in his words, but she agreed with Bramble. "It sounds like you'll have to create the drug to find a cure," she said. "That is way too risky. What if you create the drug and the man gets hold of it?"

Heath shook his head. "If I could create the drug, we'd

have the cure already. My thought is to work from the symptoms we saw and figure out what makes it happen."

"It's not something you should do alone," Fernlight said. "If something goes wrong, then no one can help."

"Nothing will go wrong," Heath said. "I'll be careful."

"You should talk to the druids first," Bramble said. "You should find out if they have any records of a spell like this."

"Can I tell them what is happening?" Heath asked.

The door to the office opened and Mamoru walked in. Fernlight held up her hand to Heath. "Wait, just a second." She looked up to Mamoru.

"You left a message," he prompted.

"Yes. We did. We have something for you," Bramble flitted back to his desk.

"Just one second," Fernlight said, turning back to Heath. "We will talk later."

"Right, I'm sure I'll have something for you when we do."

She cleared the circle.

Bramble held out his desk chair for Mamoru. "We have a report and we have two things for you." He pushed the phone and the smeared tissue toward Mamoru. Fernlight hoped that Heath's tests hadn't left a trace.

Fernlight watched their client. She needed to see his reaction to good news before giving him some bad. He was impassive, which was disappointing. They might not have much progress, but it was some, and now that they'd decided to follow Keenan, it felt less like they were stuck.

Chapter 19

"I will take these," Mamoru said, reaching into his pocket to remove two bags. "I hope we can use them to stop the drug."

Fernlight nodded to Bramble to continue.

"The phone belongs to the man we overheard. We can put it back in his house if we need to, but it's been a day, and he might have missed it by now. The stuff on the tissue is paint he was using to pretend he was magical." He paused and looked to Fernlight.

"We will follow him to see if he will lead us to the person who is creating the drug," she said.

"Is creating?" Mamoru asked.

"Yes, we have an indication that the drug is not complete," she said. *Or it is and it simply takes multiple doses to work.*

"You have other information?" Mamoru asked.

He wasn't going to let them off the hook. Fernlight took a moment to decide what to tell him first. It seemed logical that the news about the deadline would be last, it would mean not having to explain anything when she delivered it. She didn't want to tell Mamoru that they were still looking for basic clues; he might take the case elsewhere.

"If you have no more, I have my own report to make."

Fernlight took the reprieve. "Perhaps you can tell us first. It might help us to understand our findings better."

"Very well," Mamoru said. He took a small notebook from his pocket and tore out a page. Handing it to Fernlight, he said, "I have continued to search through our archives for anything that might relate to the case. The information seems to have been scattered through the database, so I have looked through many files and documents."

Fernlight looked at the paper. There was a name on it and a few details; his description, and his address.

"This caught my attention," he continued. "You may know that magical folk have been engaged by some of our larger companies. Some consulting, some research, and most of the larger pharmaceutical firms. This man was fired from Ryce-Pharma, one such firm, for unstated reasons. I did a little more checking. He was caught making meth, a highly addictive illegal drug."

"You think he's making the potion?" Bramble asked.

Fernlight looked up from the paper to see him actually hold his lips together to stop words falling out.

"Is it possible that a human could make a drug that creates magic?" Mamoru asked.

"No," Fernlight said. And then, "Maybe. We don't really know enough about human science to say for sure. If the answer is yes, then a human scientist would have to understand magic much more than I think possible."

"So, this is a wizard, or some other human-looking magical folk?" Mamoru asked.

Bramble bounced in his chair. "You don't sound like you think it could be a human either. Why did you ask? What makes you wonder? How do humans make drugs? We should have asked that before." He stopped talking when Fernlight glared at him. Then finished with, "I should let you answer before I let all of my questions out." Then he grinned.

Mamoru didn't pull back like most people when a fairy showed his teeth. It could be disconcerting even for Real Folk. Fairies seemed to have more teeth than their mouths could hold, and all of them were pointed.

"There is evidence that this drug maker could be human, but also questions about that," Mamoru said. "At least that's where our investigation led."

Fernlight was struggling to understand how a human could create a magical drug. "We all believe this is a magical source. I don't understand why one of us, the magical folk, would do it, but I cannot believe a human could create something like this. What is the evidence that the maker is human?"

Mamoru shifted in his chair. "It is a very gray area," he said. "I have researched his past and there are no records prior to the prophecy. There are many reasons why a human would change identities, but the timing is suspicious."

"How could he have created it?" Fear froze Fernlight's blood. If humans were able to create magical things, the world would become more dangerous. They didn't have the training to understand the destruction that could come from a poorly constructed spell.

"I do not understand all of the techniques used to create spells, nor do I know all of the techniques used to make medicines. But my little knowledge of magic tells me that the power, the actual magic, comes from the person. The direction for the magic comes from the ingredients, process, and intent?"

"Yes," Bramble said. "You do understand how it works." He sounded in awe of Mamoru.

The explanation did nothing to assuage Fernlight's fear. If humans could understand that in the short time they knew about the Real Folk... "And human medicine?"

"We manipulate the body's chemistry for the most part. But

we also create vaccines. This is when we inject something into a person to help them build a defense for a disease."

"Magic is not a disease!" Bramble said.

Mamoru shook his head. "I know, but is it possible that injecting a human with the blood of a magical person would transfer the magic?"

Fernlight wanted to deny it, but she didn't know enough to be sure. "I will ask our friend, Heath," she said. "Is there anything else?"

"No," Mamoru said. He seemed as shaken as she was by the thought of injecting magic.

She handed Bramble the slip of paper. "We will follow this lead. When you have finished with the phone, we can place it back where we found it. I think Keenan may not be our best lead now."

"I will not act on the information without informing you," Mamoru said. "I do not wish to tip off any of the people involved."

"We think the drug will be ready for whatever the user is going to do within the next five days," she said, then outlined why.

"I will see what I can do about identifying the attendees." Mamoru wrote a few lines in his book.

"We also saw the man who was taking the drug," Bramble said.

Mamoru jerked upright. "Then why aren't we arresting him?"

"We don't know who he is," Fernlight said. "We saw him in a summoning circle, but when we draw him, the picture smears within an hour."

"I can describe him," Bramble said. "I drew him, so I remember."

Fernlight searched her memory as she listened. The image

seemed to slip away from her every time she thought of a detail.

"He had hair," Bramble said. "It was… I can't remember. He had eyes; I can't recall the color. Wait! We wrote it down." He clicked a few keys and then fluttered away from the screen. "It's empty. The words are gone."

Fernlight turned the monitor. The file was there, but the screen was blank. "It seems the computer memory is as unstable as ours, and the pictures. What I do remember is he was able to talk to us when he should not have known we were there. And he must be rich and powerful. Keenan said something like that on the call."

Chapter 20

Mamoru left when it was clear no one had any more information and discussing the possibilities was simply wasting time.

"You didn't tell him about the cure," Bramble said as he bustled about clearing space and gathering spell ingredients. "Are we keeping secrets from our client? Is that how we do business?"

Despite the words, Fernlight heard no accusation in Bramble's tone. He was asking because he needed to know not because he disagreed. "Yes, we are keeping secrets from our client, no that is not a normal way for us to do business." She heard the contradiction in her statement. "It's complicated. The news of the cure is not really a secret. We have no cure, and if we are successful, we will only need it for one person. If we tell Mamoru now and Heath is not successful, then we are building false hope."

"I understand. It's okay to not tell something that might not help, but we shouldn't keep important information secret." Bramble seemed happy with his deduction. "But why didn't you mention the rogue wizard?"

Fernlight stopped what she was doing and turned to him. "What rogue wizard?"

"I told you. Thorn said there's a rumor that a wizard has gone rogue. Maybe he's making the drug? Why didn't you tell Mamoru?"

"Because this is the first I've heard of it. What else did she say?" Fernlight spoke quietly. The fear rising through her didn't help her think.

"I guess I forgot. I was so worried about telling you that I had shared our client information with Thorn, it just slipped my mind." He moved past her to put herbs on the table. "She only knew there was a rumor."

Fernlight felt like she was thinking through wet sand. They had the name of someone Mamoru thought was the maker. They had a rumor about something she thought would never happen. They didn't have time to follow both clues. "We'll follow this person," she said. "If it doesn't pan out, we'll ask around for more details."

"It's probably the human," Bramble said, sounding more confident than he had a right to be.

"If it isn't, we are facing a bigger danger. If any of us give the humans a legitimate reason to fear magic, they will take our freedom and probably our lives."

"It's no point worrying. We have a name, and I have everything ready for a seeker spell," he said. "Should we ask Heath if he's made any progress? It's been a long time since we talked to him."

Fernlight envied his ability to let go of his fear. She felt the kernel of it just under her heart. It wouldn't help to let fear take over. She tried to follow Bramble's example. "Let's focus on this for now. Heath may need more than a few hours to find his cure. I do not wish to slow him down with questions."

"Okay. I guess. So, we have this person's name, right?"

Fernlight checked the paper. "Zeke Middleton, and we

have his address." Fernlight placed the slip of paper on the floor next to the burn bowl.

"We could just go to his house," Bramble said. "If he's not there, we could use the tracker spell. I think Mamoru would like it better if we didn't always use magic."

It was clear to Fernlight that Bramble was feeling a little guilty about deceiving their client despite his agreement. "I don't want to track across the city if he's snug in his home."

"Do you think he's taking the drug too?" Bramble asked in a quiet voice.

Fernlight looked at her partner; he was trembling. "I hope not, why do you ask?"

"We usually remember details. If he is taking the drug, we may not be able to track him, and we may not be able to describe him. If that's true, then we can't solve the case."

Fernlight took the lighter out, ready to set fire to the spelled herbs. "I'm not sure he could be making the drug while he's going through what that man is experiencing. Let's not worry about it because we'll know soon enough."

Bramble's trembling lessened. "I will hope for success."

Fernlight placed the flame against the herbs and when smoke rose, she waved the paper through the cloud. "We seek this man."

After a few seconds, a finger of smoke pointed through their door and then broke from the cloud. Fernlight covered the spell to extinguish the fire and took her coat from the chair.

The smoke formed into a long snake of haze and swirled in a circle while they got ready.

The sun was dropping behind the tall buildings as they locked the door. Fernlight saw the cloud moving in the opposite direction to the address on the paper. "Not home," she said to Bramble. "We may be lucky and find him unprotected."

"Or it could be a trap," Bramble said. "The man could have told him about us and now they are luring us into a trap, and they are going to steal our magic. What will happen to a fairy and a sprite without magic? It will be hard to go home, and— Oh no! I have some treasure on me! He will steal it and then he can kill us without needing our magic. And then he'll find out where the rest of the treasure is." Bramble started hyperventilating.

"Why are you so determined to think of the worst?" Fernlight asked. She turned and unlocked their door. "Come, have some honey before we go."

He followed her and slumped in his chair while Fernlight took a tiny jar of honey from the shelf.

"Don't eat it all at once," she said. "We can take it with us."

Bramble slurped the honey, leaving half of it in the jar for later. "I don't know why I keep looking at the bad things. Maybe I'm cursed."

Fernlight shook her head. "Who would do that?"

"The man!" Bramble tucked the honey jar into a pocket.

"He doesn't have the knowledge yet," she said.

"How do you know?" Bramble asked. "We don't know who he is, we don't know where he is. How are you so certain that we have time?"

Fernlight secured the office and checked that the smoke track was still leading them away from the address. "Because there is no point in thinking otherwise."

She watched Bramble run that through his thoughts. His frown deepening and his eyebrows rising and falling as though each were taking opposite sides in a debate.

"Yes, you are correct. In the absence of proof that all is lost, perhaps thinking we have a chance is more productive. Maybe this not a curse, but a side effect of living on the energy meant for…" He snapped his lips closed.

Fernlight knew that the fairy treasure was vital to the health of the fairies. But only a few people knew how. Before the prophecy there was a battle with rebellious sidhe who were trying to use fairy treasure for their own purposes. No one knew how it was resolved, but the rebellion was defeated.

"I guess one thing about having a deadline," she said. "It's not going to be long before everything is resolved."

"Right! Five days... Four and a half now!" Bramble tugged on her sleeve. "Do we really have to hide the fact that we are Real Folk? We could run faster without pretending."

"Put your glamor on," she said. "We don't want curious humans to interrupt us tonight. And the human won't be moving any faster than us."

Chapter 21

Less than five days! Bramble tried to stop it but the words were ticking away the minutes in his head. The evening was proving as unproductive as all the others. They had been following the tracking spell for an hour, maybe longer, it was hard to tell the passage of time when he was concentrating on something. Okay, maybe they had made some progress, but it wasn't fast enough. If they didn't catch the man—

"Bramble, stop fretting." Fernlight drew him into the shadow of a building.

"I wasn't," he lied.

"You were mumbling. Worrying won't help. But we've found him," she said, pointing to a man standing in front of a closed store halfway down the street from them.

Bramble could see the wisp of smoke spinning above this human's head. His name was Zeke Middleton, an odd name — or maybe not for a human. No one else on the street noticed the spell. "We should capture him now and then he can't make any of the drug. It won't matter about the days if we stop him making the drug. And we can find the man who is taking the drug later."

Fernlight looked at him. He could tell she agreed with him by the struggle on her face. She knew he was right, but she didn't want to take the Zeke now. *Great! Now I'm calling him that.*

"Why not?" he asked. "We can't just let him go about destroying our future… and the future of the humans."

Fernlight touched his arm and he realized his voice was headed for ranges she wouldn't hear. He must find a way to control that when he was mad, or scared, or happy, or, well, all the time.

"We can follow him and find out where he's making the drug. Maybe we will find the man from the circle and get him arrested. We should call Mamoru!" *It was all going to work out perfectly.*

"We only suspect this is the maker. Remember, Mamoru doesn't have any proof, just a strong suspicion. And what about that rogue wizard? And remember Keenan's alarm had already been broken once before we were there, maybe that is something we should be looking into. We need to get the proof before we call Mamoru to arrest anyone."

"Why? If we are right then the problem is solved, if we are wrong, we say we are very sorry and go back to our detecting."

Fernlight kept her eyes on the Zeke. "If we are right, then great! If we are wrong, it will take time to figure out and then we are starting from the first step with less time and maybe we will have tipped off the real drug maker." She stepped out of the shadow, beckoning him to join her. "He's on the move."

Bramble followed as he tried to work out an argument that would defeat Fernlight's logic. He couldn't and that made the trembles start again. The only way to stop the shaking from making him faint was to concentrate on the man they were following.

Bramble wanted to fly up and follow the man from the air, but that would give away the fact that they were Real Folk, and it would mean they wasted time on the disguises. He tried to commit the Zeke's image to memory, afraid it would fade and jumble like the other man. This one was short, almost as short as a fairy, but not quite. And he was fat, it made him wobble a bit when he moved. Maybe he was making the drug to find a way to cast a glamor and make himself look nicer. But that would be easier if he just washed his hair and clothes, and maybe do something to style it all.

"Don't get so close," Fernlight muttered, reaching for his jacket.

Bramble was only a few feet behind the Zeke! He should be more careful. But being this close allowed him to hear the wheezing of the Zeke's breathing. *He should go to a doctor.*

Fernlight slowed their pace and then dropped back to a half block distance. The Zeke didn't even notice them.

Bramble sniffed the air and then opened his magical senses. "Fernlight, I am not sure this is the man. There is no magic in the Zeke." He tested the air again; nothing.

"I can't sense any either," Fernlight said. "Why do you call him the Zeke?"

"Isn't that his name?" Bramble wanted to get closer and touch the Zeke. Maybe there was a glamor hiding his magic.

"His name is Zeke. If you call him the Zeke it's like a title." She tugged his jacket to hold him back.

"Oh. Like my name is Bramble and I am the King, but not the Bramble." He let Fernlight keep him back. They would have time to see Zeke's magic when they arrested him. "I don't remember why I call him that. I will not do it anymore." *There are too many things to remember to fit into human society.*

"Mamoru was sure of this lead," Fernlight said. "We will stay with him until we are just as sure he is the wrong person."

"But we..." Bramble stopped talking. The Zeke was looking in a shop window again, but he kept taking peeks toward them. "The Zeke has seen us," he whispered.

"Keep going," Fernlight said. "If he only suspects us, trying to hide will confirm it. We will pass him and then we should split up. You cross the street. Can you change your glamor a little?"

They stepped into an alley in the middle of the block. Bramble rubbed the fairy treasure and set his clothing to look more ragged, and made himself taller. "Humans don't like to look at poor people," he said when Fernlight raised her eyebrow.

Bramble crossed the street, noticing that the Zeke was continuing on his walk. If they were very lucky, he would be going to the man, or to his spell workroom. Or somewhere that proved he wasn't the right person.

Across the street, Fernlight shambled from the alley. She had taken his advice and looked like she had not changed her clothes or washed for a year.

FERNLIGHT COULD SEE that Bramble was getting impatient. They had been following Zeke for a half hour and he seemed to be determined to wander through the city core for the whole night. She was tiring of the monotony as well. If he was making the drug, he didn't seem to have an urgent need to produce it. Perhaps the man they saw in the circle would be stopped simply because his supplier was too indolent to provide the means for his success.

She was currently disguised as a young woman ready to party in any of the local bars. She was glad that a change of glamor was all it took. If she really had to wear the tight clothes and high heels, it would be difficult to follow anyone.

Bramble was now sporting spiked green hair, a leather jacket and tight jeans. At five feet tall it looked a little like he was in a costume, but Zeke hadn't noticed, or at least he hadn't shown any indication of noticing. It was time to change tactics, so she caught Bramble's attention and they withdrew into a small cluttered store.

"We're closing in five minutes," a man said as they passed him.

"That's all we need," Bramble said, cheerfully.

The man waved and turned back to the book he had open on the counter.

The store contained several glass contraptions with pipes attached, a few pottery bowls and a lot of merchandise with marijuana leaves on it. There were no other stores, and this one was too small for them to hide in when they changed glamors.

"We should come back together," Bramble said. "I don't like being separate, there are too many drunken humans around, and we can't talk about what we are seeing, and I think we should consider stopping for the night, if this isn't the man, then we need to spend time finding the right one, and if it is, we can try again tomorrow."

Fernlight shifted her glamor to show a dark hoodie sweater, dark jeans and flat black shoes. "Do what I'm doing," she said. "Be quick. We don't want to have to cast a seeker spell again like last time. I only have a few more leaves for the spell and we might need it later."

Bramble flickered and then became a shorter, slighter copy of her. "But what about my suggestion? We can follow the Zeke later and—"

"No, we continue. If he's the right man, then we can't afford to let him go. What if this is the night he delivers the last of the drug? We will miss a chance to find the other man."

Bramble shrugged and marched out of the store. Fernlight followed, thanking the man behind the counter and closing the door before he looked up.

Zeke was two blocks ahead. They were entering a part of the

city that held a lot of Real Folk sites. Gastown, as the humans called it, held the sidhe court and the homes of two witches and a wizard. Since the prophecy more of the Real Folk had come to Vancouver because it was a relatively safe location. Not all places in the world were comfortable living with the presence of magic.

Banks', the Real Folk pub, was also in Gastown. They were only a few blocks away and that meant more Real Folk on the street. It gave them the cover to drop their glamors if needed.

"I don't think the man from the circle would live here," Bramble said, pointing at the rundown buildings that surrounded a few new developments. "The new homes are too small for a rich man. He would want a palace, right?"

"It's not that far from where we found Keenan," Fernlight said. "And it is probably a good place for Zeke to make a drug. I think the people who live here would keep to their own business."

Bramble glanced down the alley where Banks' door glowed faintly. "A glass of honey wine would be nice. I mean after we have followed the Zeke. Not until we are sure, of course."

Fernlight laughed. It would be nice to have a long drink of beer. "As a celebration," she said. "Look."

Ahead, Zeke turned into the deep entry to an old brick building. As they passed, Fernlight saw him fumbling with a key; beyond the door, a dimly lit lobby with a large elevator door at the back. She kept walking past and then drew Bramble to the side of the entrance. "We may have that drink soon," she whispered.

They both heard the door creak as it opened. Zeke was at his destination. She let Bramble slip past her to peek around the opening. "He is at the elevator," Bramble reported.

"We'll wait until he is on it," she said. "Then we'll go in."

Bramble nodded. "I can open the lock from here, should I do it now?"

It would speed up their entrance, and maybe allow them to

see where the elevator stopped. "Can you make sure the door doesn't come open when you do it?"

"Yes," Bramble said. Then he fidgeted with a spell. The door lock clicked. "Oops, maybe not."

He rushed forward, pulling at her jacket to follow.

As she turned to face the door, Fernlight froze. Zeke was still waiting for the elevator. He would turn and look, for sure. She couldn't say anything for fear it would alert him. Bramble was standing at the door, holding it closed with his one hand and rubbing what looked like a ruby in the other.

Zeke didn't turn.

The elevator arrived. He stepped in and pressed a button, the door closed, a bright flash of blue filled the lobby, and then they were alone.

"Did you do that? And why didn't he see us?" Fernlight asked.

Bramble put the ruby in his pocket and opened the door. "I can't tell you about fairy secrets." He wavered a little as he walked across the lobby, then collapsed.

Chapter 22

Fernlight carried Bramble from the center of the lobby and laid him on the tiled floor. She pulled the honey jar from his vest pocket and spread a drop across his lips. His tongue flicked out and within moments he was sitting up.

"Thank you," he said, quiet as a breath. Color returned to his face as he took another sip. "Next time I will bring a bigger supply."

He reached into his pocket and held something in his fist. Fernlight hoped he was not checking the contents, they needed to trust each other, and she had fought her curiosity to snoop.

"You can't sleep here," a woman said as she stepped from the shadows of a side door. "How did you get in?"

Fernlight tensed. What had the woman seen?

"We're not sleeping," Bramble said, scrambling to his feet. "We are visiting a friend in the building. How long have you been there? I mean, I'm sorry we didn't say hello." He held out his hand to shake. "I'm Bramble."

His hand was trembling. Fernlight hoped the woman would not notice. She stepped forward.

The woman looked at them, assessing whether they were

clean enough to touch, Fernlight thought. Dressed in tights, a form fitting jacket, and brightly-colored lace-up shoes, she was probably not going to a party.

She finally reached out and shook their hands. "I'm Barbara. I saw you come in as soon as Mr. Middleton closed the elevator. Were you running to catch it?"

Barbara had been in the lobby all along. Was she the reason for the blue flash? "Yes," Fernlight said. "My friend tripped over his own feet."

Bramble side stepped to the elevator and pressed the call button. "We'll let you get on your way. Have a lovely night. We are running a little late for our meeting."

Barbara looked suspicious, then at her watch. "I need to start my run now. Who are you meeting?"

"On the second floor," Bramble said. "He's very private and I'm sure he wouldn't want us to talk about him."

She began stretching her legs, then pressed a button on her watch. "Old Mr. Striatham?" She started to run in place. "Well, good luck. He's a real grouch and that dog of his barks all night."

Barbara turned right and disappeared.

"Did you see what floor the Zeke got off?" Bramble asked.

The elevator was still moving between floors. Fernlight looked at the brass counter above the door. "No, I was too worried about a fainting fairy. But we can start at the top and work our way down, see if there's a remnant of the seeker spell."

"What's wrong? I am fine, you did the right thing. Why are you frowning?"

"She was there when the light flashed." Fernlight scanned the area in front of the side door, hoping Barbara might have dropped something they could analyze.

"Do you think she might be the one making the drug?"

The brief question made Fernlight turn to look at Bramble. He was pressing the call button repeatedly. "We don't know."

A grin spread over Bramble's face. "I thought maybe she was involved. I don't think so anymore. She was too easy to fool about our presence here. If she was involved, then she would have made us leave. Or asked more questions. The Zeke created the drug. I am convinced now!"

Fernlight couldn't find any evidence of Barbara's passing through the lobby. If she could find even a small drip of water or a hair, they could test it later. "We should still be thorough. Humans are very sneaky; she could have been pretending."

The elevator dinged.

"Then it's a good thing I have this!" Bramble held up a tissue. "Come on. We need to find the Zeke."

Fernlight crossed the floor and entered the elevator. "How did you get that?"

"It was in her sleeve when we shook hands, I took it. I knew you would want to be sure she wasn't part of it. And maybe she is. We can test this later. Which floor do you want to start with? It goes to the fifth floor, But I thought the building was taller than that. Do you think we will have to find a way to get to the higher floors?"

Fernlight pressed the button for the top floor. "Let's see what's here. Maybe there are no more floors."

Bramble put the tissue in his pocket and stared at the floor indicator as they rose.

The elevator was old and it shook slightly. She could hear the mechanism groan from lack of care.

"I think we need to break into Zeke's place," Fernlight said. "We have to wait until he goes out again."

Bramble turned to stare at her. "What if he doesn't go out for hours? Days? We could put a sleep spell on him and then we could search until we released him. It's not going to hurt him, and it will be safe for us."

Fernlight didn't want to argue with Mamoru over the use of magic. Using a sleep spell to allow them to break and enter, and then steal, was a last resort. Mamoru had been more upset over the way they got the phone and cream from Keenan than happy that they had achieved something.

"Only if he doesn't go out by morning," she said.

"That's wasting time," Bramble said as the elevator doors opened. "I have another spell we can use. It will tell us how deeply he sleeps and that might let us creep in and search."

Fernlight had never heard of such a spell, but Real Folk were cagey about their most secret spells. Maybe fairies had need to know when humans would wake. They lived in human gardens after all.

"Let's find him first," she said. "Then you can show me the spell."

"You think I'm trying to sneak a sleep spell on him? I'm hurt that you don't trust me. But I'm happy that you think I am so sneaky."

There were four doors set along the hallway, each numbered. The end to the right had an exit door, and the one to the left had a door labeled 'roof'.

THE ZEKE'S home was on the second floor, on the same side as the elevator, so they wouldn't be able to look in the window from the street. The faint trace of the tracking spell blended with the carpet.

Bramble pressed his ear against the wall, but no sounds came through. "Is it possible that humans can make it sound like there is no one home?"

Fernlight shrugged. "I think we both have a lot to learn about humans."

Bramble had mixed feelings about learning. Yes, now that he knew more about Mamoru, he wasn't as terrified. But the few humans in his acquaintance were mostly bad people. It would be bad to get caught in a trap, it would be bad to leave now and not get what they need. He knew the woman, Barbara, was not involved. She didn't smell of magic, or evil. She didn't ask them too many questions, and she was more concerned with going for her run than protecting something inside the building. And he would prove that when they got back to the office. If he was alone, he would try to sneak in. If he was alone, he would cast a sleep spell. If he was alone... he wouldn't be here, because only Fernlight knew to keep looking.

"How will we know to go in?" he asked. "Or are we going to stand here until sunrise?"

He saw doubt cross Fernlight's face. She wanted to act too; he knew it. Her talk about waiting was fine when they didn't know where they were going, but now, when they were right outside the door, and maybe everything they needed was right inside, she was just as impatient as a fairy.

"Let's check the roof," she said. "If there are windows, maybe we can see what's going on."

He followed her to the stairs leading to the roof, thankful she hadn't called the elevator, which took forever to get between floors. Once in the stairwell, Bramble let his wings take over and flitted to the top of the building. The door was locked at the top, but he could take care of that.

Fernlight was right behind him and he sensed the lock and the alarm. He dealt with both, this time not melting the alarm. Stepping out he looked around. There was some kind of black sticky stuff spread over the flat roof, some equipment, and wires overhead. He couldn't see any stars because there were too many lights on the street. *Why did humans do that?*

He flew to the edge. There was no convenient garden this time. He looked down to see the building next door was only four floors high, but it almost touched this one. They would not be able to fly down and peek in the window.

Bramble noticed, that the top floor of apartments had two rows of windows. That explained why the building looked taller than it was.

Fernlight stood beside him. "Can you get between the buildings?"

"Probably, but I won't be able to hide, and I can't do the spell I did before because I don't have the energy, and we are almost out of honey."

"There are no lights," she said. "If you were careful, you could take a peek."

"I can never figure out when you want to take a risk and when you don't." Bramble climbed over the small wall at the edge of the roof. He tucked his wings in close to keep them from damage by the bricks, and inched his way down to the apartment.

When he got near the top of the window, his stupid brain reminded him of the possibility of getting caught by a real bad human and he started to tremble. He couldn't climb down any farther because his fingers wouldn't let go of the bricks.

"You have to do this," he said to himself. "Be brave." His fingers weren't listening!

Bramble looked up to see Fernlight watching. He crept up a few bricks and relaxed. Then he turned so his head was pointed at the street and went back down. His body was shaking less now that it thought he was going up. He lowered his head so that it just passed the top of the window and opened both eyes really wide to take in everything.

It was dark; the door across the room was closed. Under the window, asleep in a bed, was the Zeke.

Bramble scrambled back to Fernlight. "He is there. He is asleep. It looks like he will stay asleep. His mouth is open and he's barely moving. We should go in and search quietly and hope we don't have to go into the bedroom." He grabbed her coat and dragged Fernlight back to the stairwell.

. . .

GETTING IN HAD BEEN EASY. The Zeke didn't have a human alarm. He had a charm set into the door that would let him know if someone entered. Bramble deactivated it with a smile. The Zeke must not know that every spell has a counter.

Bramble felt very brave. He didn't faint once, and he didn't even tremble when they found the hidden door in the kitchen that took them to the apartment above. There was no furniture, only a long metal table, two metal stools and lots of pots and glasses and burners and needles and paper.

"We should get a sample," Bramble said, struggling to keep his voice quiet with all the joy bubbling up.

Fernlight shook her head. "Remember how Mamoru felt about the things we took from Keenan?"

"But we will have to come back." Bramble wandered toward the table. There was a dark blue liquid in a sealed container.

"Yes, but now we know exactly where we need to look."

Bramble pulled his fingers away from the liquid. "You can't come in through this window," he said.

Fernlight chuckled. "No, but you can, and then you can open the door for me."

Bramble flew up to the top of the window. It had only a mechanical lock. It would be easy to open.

Chapter 23

Fernlight watched as Bramble fiddled with the window. She assumed that they would be able to get back into the building since they had already come in and he could give her a spell to open the door.

"Come back down, Bramble," she said. She was still determined that they would not take anything with them but there were some things that they could do tonight.

"What are we going to tell Mamoru?" Bramble asked. "If we don't have anything to give him to test, how will we prove that we found the right person and this is the guy— the man, I guess, the Zeke — who is making their drug and if we stop him then the drug won't get out and that man won't be able to take over the world? I still don't know why somebody would want to take over the world."

Fernlight ignored Bramble's chattering. He would calm himself down eventually. They only had so much time and even though the building was solid and they could make a little noise, she didn't want to rouse Zeke from his sleep. If they could possibly spend another ten or fifteen minutes here uninterrupted, she could cast some spells to identify what was in the blue glowing container. One of the things that she could cast was a separation spell; it was often how counter spells were developed in the forest. And it was how they sometimes had to discover what had been spilled or poured into the dark places in the forest in order to remove the poisons that the humans had dropped there.

"Bramble, be careful around those glasses, we don't want to break anything. Do you have any rosemary with you?" Fernlight dug in her bag to find some packets of spider dust, ground opals, and her lighter.

Bramble handed her a few spikes of rosemary that had been cleaned off the branch. They wouldn't be able to cast the spell more than once. If they were unsuccessful, they could come back with more ingredients.

"You are going to try and filter these ingredients, that's a good idea, I should've thought of that. Maybe if we can get it done tonight, we can have Heath give us a prepared package. It is a good idea that would be an efficiency that he could create. He would be very happy to know that information, I will remember to tell him." Bramble was staring at the closed container, his hand reaching dangerously close to it.

Fernlight cleaned an area next to the container and laid out her ingredients. "I've never done this without a real sample," she said. "Any ideas?"

Bramble tipped his head to the side and stared at the liquid inside the jar. Then he leaned forward and sniffed at the seal. Then he placed his hand above the seal, testing for heat. "The seal is very tight, but I can smell something. But if we want to be sure we could open the seal just a little, tiny tiny tiny tiny bit."

Fernlight shook her head. "We don't know if he's used some kind of spell that would indicate that we've opened it. The only thing I can think of is to put the jar on the spell ingredients, which means that we have to move it. We have to put it back exactly the way it was, Bramble."

"I will remember, fairies are good at remembering." His eyes got wide. "Unless this is like the man, what if it shifts and changes, what if we can't put it back—"

Fernlight put up her hand to stop the rambling. "Is there any way to test that?"

Bramble put his hands on his hips and stared at the glass container. "I am memorizing it. I will fly back up to the roof. And I will draw it there. Then I will bring my drawing back. And we will see if I have it right."

Without waiting for Fernlight to agree, Bramble rushed to the window, flicked open the lock, and disappeared. Fernlight waited, holding her breath. She did not like being alone with all of this bad magic. The longer they stayed the more she felt pressure on her skin like something was sorting out what was magic about her and what was not magic. Was this something to do with the spell that Zeke was compiling?

She had not finished her worrying when Bramble returned to the room with a sheet of paper rolled in his hand. He opened it up without speaking and placed it on the counter. The jar was depicted completely as it was in real life.

"We have some luck," Fernlight said.

Standing carefully over the container, Fernlight laid out the ingredients of the spell in a circle around it. The magic they would use was simple, mostly because they did not want the spell to contaminate the results. She bruised the rosemary and the room started to smell clinical and clean. The ground opals shimmered as she smeared them in front of the container. Then she took the spider dust and sprinkled it in the air saying the words of the spell. "I ask that you tell me the magic of this item. I have no harm in my heart."

She moved back and watched as the spider dust formed a screen in front of the jar. The opal powder rose to paint the screen, and the oil from the rosemary pooled in circles upon the opal sheen.

"It didn't work. We knew it was magic. It's not telling us what is happening." Bramble flew around the jar, careful not to disturb the spell.

Fernlight closed her eyes and sent her focus to the spell one more time. "Let the oil represent the mundane, let the gems represent the magic, present them in a manner that we may know the makeup of the spell."

She opened her eyes to see the ingredients of the spell moving on the dust screen. The oil slid to the bottom and then rose up the sides creating almost a bowl for the opalescence of the gems. Just as she was sure that the analysis was complete, the entire thing reversed.

"What do you think that means? Did it help us? I don't think it did." Bramble settled beside her to stare at the screen.

Fernlight was about to say she didn't know, when the screen changed again. This time the rosemary oil and the opalescence mixed together.

"This is why it is not yet ready," she said. "See how it fluctuates. Much like the man in the vision. I think it means we have more time."

"It doesn't matter. We only have a few days, remember. That event is going to happen soon," Bramble said.

Chapter 24

After leaving Zeke's laboratory, Fernlight did not want to go back to the office. It was too late to call Mamoru, but Heath should be awake.

"Maybe he has already found a cure," Bramble said. "I know he said he would call us, I know it could take a long time, but we had so much luck tonight, maybe there is more luck available, and we could find the man who took it and give him the cure and then he wouldn't want the drug anymore."

Fernlight wasn't sure that Bramble's reasoning was solid, but she liked the idea of them having more good luck. Finding the lab had been a success, but it would have been nice not to have restrictions placed on them by Mamoru. If it had just been her, she would have sought Beacon's advice, but that would have been with Zeke at her side in the dark parts of the forest. "Even if Heath doesn't have a cure yet, he will be happy to know what we found. And it might help."

Heath's home was not that far from where they had found Zeke's laboratory. Vancouver, at least downtown Vancouver, wasn't that large. The street seemed normal; dark, quiet, and slightly menacing.

Bramble ran ahead and started knocking on Heath's door. Fernlight followed, reached above his head, and knocked harder. "If he's in the middle of a spell, he may not hear us."

The door opened. Heath stood inside smiling, looking as though he hadn't slept since they last saw him, or combed his hair.

"I am not in the middle of a spell," he said. "I needed to stop for some tea. Come on in, I'll make you a pot and we can chat."

That would be nice. Fernlight suddenly felt parched and realized she hadn't had anything to eat or drink for hours. And she had not refreshed her magic for days.

When they were all sitting comfortably in Heath's messy room, Fernlight gave him an update on what they had found.

"That's just great," Heath said. "I am kinda stalled. I think that there is actually a cure. I mean logically there should be a cure; every spell has a counter spell. At least that's how it's worked up 'til now. But I can't figure out what the components are." He looked at them as though expecting more.

"We didn't bring any," Bramble said. "Because we think, well, Fernlight thinks, that Mamoru would be angry. Remember he was pretty angry. Oh, you weren't there. He didn't like the fact that we took stuff from Keenan's house. He said maybe that the authorities, I guess he means the police, would think that we had contaminated things with our magic."

Heath sat back, surprised. "But how am I going to analyze the contents of the spell without some of the spell?"

Fernlight couldn't answer his question. Her concern at the lab had been Mamoru's need for clean evidence. She should have thought about the cure or that Heath might be able to identify the real components of the spell. They still didn't know what Zeke was using to put the magic into it that could be transferred to a human.

"We could go back," Bramble said. "If we go now, we

could come back before morning. It's not too late. He might still be asleep. Or he might be out. He's probably not inside his lab. Well, at least we should look."

Breaking in twice in one night seemed overly risky, but this was a dire situation. "It won't be that easy, Bramble. What if that woman comes back from her run to find us breaking into the building again?" She didn't really want to argue him out of going there, but this time they needed to know how they were going to handle all eventualities. The last thing that they needed that night was Bramble having another fainting attack because he'd used up his energy.

Before Bramble could answer, Heath broke in and said, "I have another idea. It's not sure, and I'm basing it on more conjecture than any evidence."

Fernlight could feel her tolerance for blabbering starting to wear thin. Between Bramble and now Heath it seemed to take twice as long to get any information out. The days were slipping by and they only had about three left. And even more importantly, the night was slipping by. At some point, it would be too risky to go back. She waited for Heath to speak, glaring at Bramble to keep him from interrupting.

"I think I know why we can't remember the man's face, or keep a picture stable." Heath looked at them as if waiting for them to provide the answer. When neither of them spoke, he continued, "it's because he's neither magic nor human. Until he settles into one, he isn't real in either."

"What is your intuition on what will happen when he becomes magic?" Fernlight asked.

"Yes," Bramble said. "Even when he's had all the magic drug, he won't be magical; he won't be a Real Folk. But he won't be a human either, does that mean he will be invisible to us?"

Heath rubbed his forehead, clearly thinking about the question. "I hadn't thought that far. But it's a good question. I don't have a gut feeling about it. Let's hope we never have to find out."

This case was getting heavier and heavier with everything they found out. Humans had enough problems accepting Real Folk, but a human with magical power? One who might be impervious to tracking spells? Fernlight wondered if perhaps the man's plans would come to fruition just because he was a new creature.

"We can't spend all our energy worrying about things that we can't understand. Our goal is still to stop this drug taking effect." Fernlight stood. "Come on, Bramble, we'll talk about how to get into the building on the way there."

"Remember what I said inside the lab," Bramble reminded her. "Before we go let's see if Heath has a better invisibility spell. That will save us some time, and some energy. Speaking of which, Heath, you have any spare honey?"

Chapter 25

They were standing back in Zeke's lab. Fernlight looked around for any evidence that they'd been noticed or that anyone else had been in the room. It looked identical to the way they had left it. The knot of worry that her nerves had tied themselves into loosened a little, but didn't go away.

Bramble was securing the lock on the window that he had flown in through — their original plan working perfectly. She hoped their luck would hold, but knew it could change quickly, and was determined it would not be changed through their own actions. Staying nervous meant she stayed alert. The fact it drew her energy faster was not important right now.

"Did you look before to find out if there were any bags of ingredients anywhere?" Bramble asked. "If we can take a little of the ingredients, then it might be better. I'm scared that if we take some of this potion, it might get on us, and it might have a bad effect on us. And what if I was not a fairy anymore?"

Fernlight looked around her. There were very few places where Zeke could store the ingredients he needed. "Are there any alarms on the lockers? or on those bins?"

She watched Bramble hovering over each of the potential

places. Each time he passed his hand over the latch, or seal, he shook his head. She couldn't tell whether the head shake meant there was no alarm, or that he couldn't tell, or that he was amazed that there was no lock on such important items.

Bramble returned to her side. "I can sense no alarms, but that doesn't make sense. It's not like he made it hard for us to find the lab. But maybe he wasn't expecting us to find him. So, he's cocky. That will work in our favor." As he said the last word, his eyes got wide. "OR IT COULD BE A TRAP!"

Fernlight was thankful that Bramble had enough control to only whisper-shout the last line. "Don't even think that. If it was a trap, we would have tripped it last time we were here." *Or at least I hope so.*

"How much time do you think we have?" Bramble asked as he started to open some of the containers on the table. "If we could search the whole place, I bet we would find everything we need. Maybe even a cure, because who would make a drug like this without a cure?"

Fernlight had no answer for that. No Real Folk would do it, but who knew what a human would resort to.

She watched Bramble closely for a few minutes, ensuring that in his eagerness to find information he didn't spill, break, or misplace anything that would give away their presence.

"I don't know how long we have," she said. "I really don't know any more than you do. We should try to do this in as little time as possible. If we haven't found anything in a couple of minutes, we should concentrate on getting a sample of the contents of the jar. We need something to hold it. Have you seen any smaller jars, or something to take our sample? I don't think either of us should be touching it even with gloves on."

Bramble put the metal container he was looking into back on the table. "A spoon and a container. We should've thought to bring it from Heath's. I'll check the cupboards." He looked back at her and saw something in her expression. "I'll be careful. I'll be quiet. Don't worry."

Fernlight let Bramble continue with his work on the storage containers. She felt drawn to the jar that sat glowing blue in front of her. She knew that was probably part of the magic. Ignoring it she walked around the table, searching for anything that might help them. At the far end, a drawer had been built into the table. It was locked, but it was a simple mechanism, and she was able to open it without Bramble's help, or leaving any marks.

Inside was a pile of notebooks and a variety of pens and pencils. She carefully lifted the books onto the tabletop. Opening each one in turn she found all but the bottom one blank. Inside that one was notes that were clearly labeled 'magic drug'. That was the only clear thing about them. The notes themselves were written in some kind of code. It was intricate and the passage was far too long for Fernlight to create a copy. If necessary they would come back a third time.

Bramble flitted back to the table to stand beside Fernlight. He looked at the pages she held open. "I could memorize that if we had time. Do you want me to try to memorize any of it? Do you think it would be worthwhile having even a little fragment of it for Heath?"

Fernlight closed the book. "We'll tell him about it when we return with the sample. I don't want to get distracted. Did you find anything?"

Bramble opened his hands to show two knives; one with the blade forming a triangle at the top, the other a more normal-looking blade. Both had been honed until they were thin on the cutting edges. "If we use one of these to open the jar, it might not show. I checked, it looks like it's just wax around the edge, we could reseal it very, very easily. And I found these," Bramble opened his other hand. A small long-handled spoon, and a thin vial with a cork in the end. "There is some very sticky tape there too, we can use that to seal the vial."

Fernlight took the instruments from Bramble. This is going to take a very steady hand, and a lot of concentration. "Warm some of the wax while I get the sample."

She made sure the drawer was locked, and then returned to the place where the jar seemed to be waiting just for her. She took the knife with the triangle blade and carefully sliced the seal of wax. The siren song of the jar became stronger. Fernlight closed her mind to the lure. Wishing she had some protection for her hands, she touched only the top of the cork, and gingerly tugged until the jar was open. An aroma of the forest filled her senses, making her long for home. She laid the lid carefully on the table.

"It smells like ripe berries," Bramble called across the room.

Fernlight stopped moving. This spell was not something a Real Folk would have created. What she thought was like the forest could not also carry the scent of berries. The spell seemed to know what they each valued the most. Fernlight took the spoon and, even though the contents of the jar were less than an inch below the lid, she wished that the handle were twice as long. Taking a spoonful she poured it into the vial and held the vial up. The blue liquid seemed to wrap itself around the inside of the glass. There was room for another spoonful, but Fernlight wanted the jar closed and its heady fragrance contained. To do that, she needed to put the vial down. Looking at the space, Fernlight realized she had not made preparation for placing the vial open on the desk. If she placed it down now, it might spill and there would be a mark.

She looked back to see Bramble carrying a bowl of wax toward her, keeping his eyes on the contents. He placed it on the table and then looked at her.

"Oh," he said. "It's calling my name. I don't want to answer. What do I do?"

Fernlight could hear the same fear in his voice that she felt in her heart. "Close the jar or take the spoon."

Bramble looked between the two options, then reached with trembling fingers for the spoon.

"Don't put it down," Fernlight said. "I'm not sure we'll be able to clear it up."

Between them, they placed the lid on the jar, the cork in the vial, and repaired the wax seal.

"What will we do with the spoon?" Bramble asked. "We can't take it with us, we'll get that on us. If we clean it, what will we do with the rag?"

Fernlight knew that they couldn't just leave the spoon as it was. There was a slick of the blue liquid on the bowl. They didn't know enough about the spell to know how to dispose of the evidence. She slipped the vial in her bag. "What if we burn it?"

Bramble looked up at her then at the spoon. "We don't know if the spell will spread by burning. But there isn't any other way. Unless…" He dashed back to one of the lockers. Then returning with yet another jar, he said, "we could put it in this. It's acid. There must be a way he cleans his instruments. I think it's this. But we have no choice."

He opened the jar and the acidic fumes bit the back of Fernlight's throat. She held her breath, dipped the spoon in, and watched as the blue slick bubbled away into nothing.

Chapter 26

When she placed the vial in Heath's hand, Fernlight felt relief flood her and untie the knots in her nerves. Not that having Heath contaminated would be a good thing, but at least it would not be her.

"Is it enough?" Bramble asked. "It was very dangerous, we tried very hard not to get caught, and I think we did okay, but it won't be any good if you don't have enough to test."

"It should be plenty," Heath answered.

Fernlight watched him hold the vial to eye level. Even now she could still feel it calling her, what was it like for a wizard?

"I've never seen anything like it," he said, his voice awed. "Was it like this with all of the potion? How did you resist?"

Fernlight thought before she spoke, he hadn't meant how had she resisted really, he had meant how did she find the strength to do so. "I thought about how awful it would be if I allowed it to take me. It helped a little. What are you going to do?"

Heath led them into his back room. "Let's hope the circle protects us from this," he said. "It should, after all the man was not able to penetrate the protection. As to what I'm going to do, I need to test it against a solution that I created that might possibly be a cure."

He hadn't mentioned that the last time they were here; had he suddenly just found the solution? Fernlight did not enjoy the feeling of suspicion that rose within her. As her distrust of Heath grew, the call of the vial became stronger.

"It is far from perfect," he admitted. "I was almost there when you were here earlier. But I was stuck, and even if this isn't a cure, testing it will take me closer, or at least give me a new direction to search in."

Bramble flew around Heath as though he was drawn to the vial. Fernlight reached to pull him back toward her and ground him within the circle, but he flitted out of the way.

"Will you use it all?"

The lack of follow-on questions worried Fernlight. "We destroyed some with acid," she said.

"Yes. I asked because I don't want this in any form around us Real Folk. You have to be very careful, Heath. It could hurt us." Bramble moved away from the vial and settled on the ground.

Heath placed the vial in a pottery bowl, cork facing down. Then he set the circle of salt. "I agree. I think I have enough here to run three tests, but if any remains, even the coating on the vial, I will ensure it's destroyed." He looked up from the vial. "Oh, I should've asked if you wanted to stay before I closed the circle."

Fernlight needed to be there. She looked at Bramble, who shrugged.

"Let's get on with it, Heath." She wanted the vial destroyed as quickly as possible.

Heath reached into a box that had been sitting in the center of the circle when they arrived. Pulling out three saucers and three small sachets of herbs, he placed them on the ground. Then he took some oil from a small cruet and poured a little into each saucer. "The oil is to help mix together all of the ingredients," Heath said. He pointed to the middle saucer. "In this one I will place only the solution that you brought. This will tell us how it interacts with the oil."

Heath reached for the vial, but didn't open it yet. "In the saucer on the right, I will combine the solution with what I think is my cure. And in the final saucer I will place my cure without the solution in case we need more tests."

Fernlight watched Heath's hands as he spoke. Inside she was torn between fascination and terror.

"How will you know that the cure has worked?" Bramble asked. "And what about the oil, won't it dilute the magic in the spell?"

Heath nodded as though he were a teacher quietly praising a bright student. "The oil is unlikely to have an effect. There is very little of it, although I suppose compared to the sample we received it seems like a lot. This is a common way of testing spells. As to the cure, knowing it works? If it reacts at all, we will consider it a success. What I can do with that reaction is use the control saucers to further test and narrow the results."

Fernlight's patience was drying up. This day seemed to be taking a week to pass. "Perhaps we should keep our questions until after the test." She glanced at Bramble to ensure that he did not take offense.

He nodded at her. "When we see the results, we'll know what to ask."

Heath swallowed, and Fernlight was somewhat pleased to see he was as nervous as she was. He took the vial and drew from his pocket a set of tweezers. Using them he pulled the vial cork free and tipped a single drop into two of the test saucers. Then he corked the vial again and placed it gently back in the bowl. Taking one of the packets of herbs, he placed a tiny pinch in the test saucer, and a similar amount in the final one.

Nothing happened. Fernlight looked up at Heath, but he

seemed unconcerned. She closed her lips to avoid asking questions since this did not seem to be the end of the test.

Heath placed his hand over the saucer containing both cure and solution. "Join together these two opposing forces." Light fell from his hand and touched the saucer.

The two liquids in the saucer came together, sliding over the pool of oil. As they came together a flame raced along the thin line of oil between them. The herbs burned. The blue potion did not change.

"Not good." Heath carefully scooped the blue solution off the top of the oil and placed it back in the vial. Then he cleared the other saucers.

Despite her earlier curiosity, Fernlight had no questions to ask.

"Did it work? That seems very anticlimactic. But perhaps it didn't work? But if it didn't work what will we do now?" Bramble asked.

Heath completed the spell clearing rituals and lifted the salt circle. "We continue as we have been doing," he said.

"We don't have enough time to start from the beginning," Fernlight said.

Chapter 27

Heath stared at the vial in his hand. "Do we know how the man from the circle takes the drug?"

Bramble sorted through his memories of what had happened in the case so far. It was fortunate that the only thing that seemed elusive was the way the man looked. "We saw him inject something, but remember we thought it was to stop the symptoms," Bramble said. "Mamoru mentioned something about vaccinations. I would expect that it would be injected or tasted. Unless it is formed into a pill. How else do people take drugs? How else do we pass on spells? For us it's usually drinking a potion, or burning and inhaling the smoke, or carrying something that has been charmed and breaking, squeezing, or rubbing it."

Heath held up the vial to the wizard light that now burned in the center of the room. "We don't have enough to test all of those methods."

Bramble looked to Fernlight hoping that she would know what to say. He feared that Heath was going to test the potion on himself. Fernlight's expression matched his own feelings.

"You cannot test this on yourself," she said, echoing Bramble's thoughts.

Heath turned away from staring at the blue liquid, Bramble knew what he was feeling. The potion called to all of them. But it seemed stronger for the wizard.

"We need a cure, right? Do you have any other ideas? Do we have time?" There was eagerness in Heath's voice. "One dose won't hurt. But I will taste the components. It is not unheard of in our practice. All apprentice wizards learn to guard against things going wrong in this process. It is one of the first lessons we learn."

"But we don't know what it will do to you." Bramble scrambled for ways to talk Heath out of it. "And what if it does something bad, and you leave this room and then you become like the man and you'll want to take over the world? Are we strong enough to stop you?"

Heath began to work the vial cork clear of the glass. "We don't need to worry about that. I will set the salt circle with the string. You will be outside observing. If something bad happens, leave the circle in place and go bring Lionel, or Quinn Larson, to deal with it."

Bramble felt his heart speed up. Wizards were supposed to be the rational ones. If they had to go and get someone to fix Heath's mistake, they would be wasting time. He mustn't faint. He lowered himself to the floor as soon as he realized he was about to bump his head on the ceiling. When he looked up again his heart was slower, but that didn't last long. Fernlight was pushed against the wall by an invisible hand, the same one forcing him to slide along the floor to the wall. Heath was turning in a circle casting the salt string only inches beyond his own body.

Bramble struggled toward him trying to stop him from closing the circle. But he was too late. The force of the protection bounced him back against the wall. He fell to the floor again, bruising his wings.

"Watch him carefully," Fernlight said. She slumped away from the wall as the protection circle was complete and the force released them. "I'm going to set a second circle. I don't trust this newfangled salt string. And if he can pass through the first circle, or break it, he will not be able to open mine."

Bramble ignored Fernlight as she took a box of salt from the corner of the room and started to walk in a larger circle around the wizard. Heath didn't waste any time. As soon as he was sure that they could not enter his circle, he tipped the contents of the vial into his mouth.

Bramble waited, his imagination feeding him visions of the wizard crumbling away to dust, or bursting into flame, or turning blue, or shriveling up. What actually happened was nothing. Well, not quite nothing. He seemed to feel something because he rubbed his hands across his stomach. But it couldn't have been much, because he didn't even scrunch his face up.

Heath looked out and met Bramble's eyes. Then he shrugged and moved his hands as though casting a spell.

It is too soon to open the circle. But that was not what Heath was doing. He held out his hand and muttered some words that Bramble could not hear. Then he leaned in, staring at the palm of his hand.

"Fernlight, what is going on? I think he's trying to cast magic. But it's not working."

"I'm not opening the circle until I know for sure."

Bramble flitted around the edges of the circle. It was good that Heath had drawn his so close to his body because there was room to maneuver. He waved at Bramble and pointed to the floor. Bramble hovered and watched as Heath pulled out a stick from his pocket; it was a piece of willow. Something that the wizard would burn to make a spell go somewhere. But all Heath did was write on the ground.

Magic gone. Heath looked up and Bramble nodded that he had read it. Heath used his foot to smooth the dirt. *You need to open the circle.* He looked up and Bramble shook his head, pointing at Fernlight. They both turned to look at Fernlight.

Fernlight tried to shout through the protection spells. "Too dangerous."

Heath put his hand to his ear, indicating he hadn't understood or heard. She searched around the corners of the room. Finding nothing she held up a finger and left the room. Before Bramble could panic, she returned with a stick in her hand.

She wrote, *it's too dangerous, we don't know what will happen.* Then she looked at Heath.

No risk. I know something, he scratched into the dirt.

"This is too hard," Bramble said. "If his magic is gone, why can't we let him out? He can't do any damage. And maybe what you can do is just make a break in the salt string."

Fernlight kept her eyes on Heath as she spoke. "Heath can do us no damage, I agree. But what if our magic disappears?"

Bramble hadn't considered that. When Heath lost his magic, he kind of became human. Wizards and witches and Druids were all like humans so they might turn into them. But Fernlight was a sprite. Would she turn into a tree? And what was a fairy underneath the magic? Was he just magic? His heart started to beat fast again. He flew closer to Fernlight in case he fainted. He felt safer next to her. And his heart slowed down a little.

IMPORTANT NEWS. Heath was stamping his foot and pointing at the words in the ground.

"He wouldn't be doing that if it wasn't important. If we keep him there, he will not damage anyone, but it's not healthy for him." Bramble tugged at Fernlight's jacket. "Just make a gate in your circle. Let me in. And I will open gate in the inner circle. Then I can find out what the news is. And I can assess Heath. And I can tell you whether it's safe or not."

Fernlight stepped to the edge of her circle. "I think it's still risky. I'll open the gate, you go in, and I'm closing the gate in the circle. Do you still want to go?"

Bramble's fear screamed NO! Fernlight was right, this was very, very dangerous. But if they were going to save the Real Folk and the humans from this drug, he had to take the chance. He trusted Heath. And Heath wasn't flickering. "Yes."

Fernlight opened a gate in her circle by brushing aside some of the salt. Before he could change his mind, Bramble slipped inside the space. He turned to see Fernlight already filling the circle. "Wait. If it is safe I'm going to need a signal. I guess I need one if it's not safe too. Unless Heath eats me. Then you will know."

Fernlight snorted a laugh. "It may not be as obvious as being eaten. If it is safe, or at least you think it's safe, then wave your hands. If it is not safe, come back to this point after closing the circle behind you and I will let you out. You must move as fast as a fairy can move."

I hope that is faster than a wizard without magic can move.

Bramble moved a quarter turn around the circle, to where Heath had crossed the ends of the string. He looked up. The wizard was watching him carefully, but he didn't look dangerous. Not even dangerous like a human. Bramble used his toe to push the salt string aside just enough to let him in. And then restored it behind him.

"I was afraid to touch it," Heath said. "I guess I would have eventually."

It is nice not to be the only frightened person in the room. "What is your news? I mean tell me your news, and then we'll decide whether it's safe to let you out. But we won't leave you here alone. We will get Quinn Larson, or Lionel, or even Dionne. They can come and they can try to heal you. So probably Dionne would be best because she is a healer."

"I can describe the man in the circle," he said. "I think it's because I'm neither magic nor human right now. I think I have a way of keeping the information set. So you can take it to your client."

"Tell me what it is, and I will go and ask Fernlight to let you out."

"I can't tell you, because it might slip from your mind. I need things that are in my front room. You have to let me out."

Bramble flew toward Heath's face. It didn't seem like he was trying to fool them. But Bramble needed to look in his eyes. He was afraid to touch the wizard. In case whatever had stolen his magic would transfer to him. But there was nothing in Heath's eyes that said he was trying to fool them. Bramble had to decide. He looked back at Fernlight who was watching closely. Then he raised his arms and waved his hands.

Chapter 28

Fernlight placed the printed list on the desk. Heath's idea seemed to have worked. It was almost an hour since they wrote the list and it still remained clear and complete.

Losing his magic had not diminished Heath's curiosity. As soon as he was free from the circle, he dove into the textbooks and articles piled around the living room. Before they'd left, she'd contacted Quinn Larson, the wizard who changed the world with one prophecy, and he had agreed to visit Heath that evening.

"This is very heartening," Bramble said. "I think that we should try to get Mamoru here now, because it might not last. Before you say anything, I know it's very late, but maybe he will be awake and come. Because last time we had information and he didn't come."

"It's worth a try," Fernlight said. She left Bramble to make the phone call and sat at his computer. Her earlier lessons came back to her, so she started typing.

"He answered the phone, he's coming right over. What are you doing?"

165

Fernlight finished typing into the search bar before answering. "It occurred to me, that if the thing we saw with this man is actually happening and not simply a reflection of his magic, he may not be in the public eye right now. It would be very hard to keep a secret like that. And we would have seen that information in one of the searches we did before." She sat back and allowed Bramble to see the screen.

"You are searching for people who haven't been seen? That is a very strange search request. But you have lots of responses."

"Is there a better way to ask the question, or is it simply the search that won't work?" There were no responses on the screen to her question; they all referred to celebrities and old mysteries. And that had not happened earlier when Bramble was doing the typing.

Bramble reached for the keyboard, pulling it from her hands. "Now that we have a description, maybe we should search for news articles about people with all of these attributes. And if we find an article that says they haven't been around for a while, that might be our person. But if they're not really in the public eye a lot, then maybe no one would have noticed that they aren't around right now. And if they're not around, how are they arranging these big events that we saw?" He checked the list again and then ran his finger across the search bar. "Short red hair, green eyes, man."

The response was immediate, but far too many, and some were women, and others had black hair. None of the images that came up were of their man. Fernlight wondered how she knew that. She still couldn't remember the details of his face, but she knew that none of these pictures were right.

Bramble huffed in impatience. "I am going to make one of the old searches happen again, and then we can look at those pictures instead of trying to look at too many red-haired, green-eyed men."

Fernlight left him to it. She trusted that when he had a small enough group of searches he would call her over. She needed to refresh her power, if only a little. A block away there was a park where she could place her feet in the dirt. "I will be back soon. If Mamoru shows up first, please keep him busy."

Bramble made an acknowledging noise, but kept his eyes on the screen in front of him.

Fernlight ran to the park. There was no one around to see how quick she was, and in this neighborhood they knew she was Real Folk anyway. Thinking of the neighborhood made her remember the promise to Bella to join her at one of the business owners' meetings. And perhaps, if Mamoru had no information, Bella would know who the man was. She was a businesswoman, he was a businessman, they would likely know of each other.

At the park, she slipped out of her shoes, stepped over the edge of a planter, and sank her feet into the ground. She could feel the life of the tree and the small plants that were contained in the planter. Very faintly, she could hear the life of the forest, and the strong flow of life of the world. She stood for only five minutes, not wanting to take any vitality from the plants, but the shock of what had happened had depleted her power too much to ignore.

When she stepped out, she realized she should have brought something to wipe her feet, they were too dirty to put into her shoes. She picked up her shoes and ran back to the office. A block away she saw Mamoru approaching. She ran inside, wiped her feet, slipped on her shoes, and alerted Bramble.

Mamoru opened the door to the office and stepped inside. It was the part of the night where most humans were asleep, yet Mamoru looked as fresh and rested as he did during the day.

"I hope this time you have proof, or more concrete information." He sat on the client chair, crossed his arms and waited.

"Have you been able to get any information from the phone?" Bramble asked.

"It has not been that long since you gave me the phone."

Fernlight did not want to sit and wait while Bramble made his way around to the information. "The last time we spoke we were not able to give you any information on what this man looked like. The man who was taking the drug. Something has happened that we prefer not to tell you, it is not illegal. Now we have, not a description, but a list of his characteristics. We are trying to determine who he is."

"If I can help I will. But if all you have is a list, then I'm not sure how I am to determine who this man is from all of the human beings here."

Bramble took one of the copies of the list and handed it to Mamoru. "Here it is. I have tried to search for him online, but I have been unable to create a question for the spirits of the Internet to be able to answer. We know that he is a business-man. We think perhaps..." Bramble paused to look at Fern-light; she nodded for him to continue. "We think that maybe he is not being seen. If his real body is acting in the way that his spirit body from the circle is acting, then he would not want to be where others can see him. And we would not have to search for his identity. I think it would be very much in the news."

Mamoru looked at the list, his brow furrowing in a frown. "Do you remember anything else?"

"If we did, it would help us find him. But some part of this drug pulls his image out of our minds almost as soon as we try to find it. The only thing I think that is not on the list, and it is not part of his appearance, is the way he spoke. His words were clipped as though he couldn't bear to take the time to finish speaking them. And when he looked at me, it was as though I could feel it on my skin."

"I think I know who it is. I cannot believe it of this person. Although, there is a part of me that knows this is true. He is a very powerful man. You will need to bring absolute proof of his guilt. And you must do it fast. If he finds that you are seeking him, he will react, and you will not fare well."

Fernlight watched Bramble begin to tremble. It would not be good for business to have their clients see what happened when a fairy became terrified. She caught his eye, and then glanced at the seat, which he was now floating a foot above. Sitting down seemed to calm him.

"If you know who he is," she said, noticing a tremble in her own voice. She cleared her throat and continued, "why do you not simply arrest him yourself?"

Mamoru pressed his lips together and then moistened them. He looked to Bramble, who was now settled and not trembling, and then to Fernlight. "I will arrest him if you can give me proof. This man is one of the leaders of my organization. He is successful with his own business, and influential at HOP-D. I am used to trusting his advice. But he does have a very large ego, and little patience. And your description matches him."

Since their first sight of the man, the drug taker, Fernlight had assumed it was a powerful human. Mamoru's clear fear of confronting the man only made her feel more determined to stop what was coming. "Tell us his name. And where he lives, and anything else you know, and we will get you your proof."

"His name is Talbot Ryce. You are correct about him not being in public. He has not attended any meetings of the board of HOP-D for a month. He has not missed one in the five years we have been in existence. I do not know about his own company, but it is simple to run your business without being there in person." Mamoru stood and straightened his jacket. "I will provide you with his office address. And I will find his home address. He is a very private person, so that may take some time. And he is very rich, so he may have more than one home."

Chapter 29

An hour later, Fernlight stood with Bramble on the street. They looked up at the tall building across the road. Mamoru had sent them the address of Talbot Ryce's office, and suggested that if they needed to search, they should do it now. He said that the cleaners would be finished, and the security would be lax. Or as lax as it would be at any point during the day.

"Do you think it's hot in there? I mean during the day when the sun is out. How do they get any work done?" Bramble asked.

Fernlight didn't really care how much work was done during the day. This building was like the others around it — almost completely constructed of glass panels. Humans seem to like the look, but when they were in his office, Fernlight would be too far away from the ground for her liking.

"Do you have any more of Heath's invisibility spell?" Fernlight asked. She saw no other way of entering the building.

Bramble dug through his bag, brought out a small sachet and held it up to her. "Not much, but if we are careful it should be enough to get us in and out. If we stay too long, it may be that we will start to fade back into visibility again."

Fernlight glanced across the street at the two men behind the counter. They were talking to each other, but there was no way they would miss a six-foot sprite and a fairy walk past them to the elevators. They couldn't climb up because the glass wouldn't give purchase, and the building was too high for Bramble to fly over. "We need to test it. Get just enough ready to apply to you, and stay behind me until we reach the building. Before we go in the door, apply the spell. If the guards see two of us, then we will have to come up with another plan."

Fernlight walked in front of Bramble. There was no need to alert the guards inside that something was up by having him disappear at the door, but she didn't want to waste the spell on crossing the street. At such a small dose, there could be an effect on the duration.

The guards were more alert than she originally thought. As soon as it was clear she was coming to the building, one of them approached the door, and pressed a button on the wall.

"Is there something I can help you with?" The voice came out of a box set to the right of the door.

Bramble danced around from behind her and started flying at the man and waving his hands. It worked. The guard didn't react, just looked at her with a questioning expression.

"I was supposed to meet a friend here," she said. "She was part of the cleaning crew and I thought she'd be coming out by now."

The guard took his hand off the button and turned to say something to the other man. Fernlight took the moment to grab Bramble's arm and move him behind her again.

The voice came out of the box again. "The crew left an hour ago. They wouldn't come through the front anyway."

Fernlight looked around as though she expected the 'friend' to appear. "Maybe she's waiting for me."

"Not a great place to hang out at this time of the night, but all services and deliveries go through the rear door." He nodded his head to the left. "It's fastest to go around the side of the building. You'll see the alley. The service door is halfway down." He continued to look at her. Was he expecting another question?

"Thanks, I'll go look. I'm sure she's there."

He frowned. "I don't like the idea of you going there alone. I can't leave. I could check the camera."

Camera? That meant they couldn't just break the lock and disable the alarm. Fernlight took her phone out and looked at the screen. "You were right. She's at the bar already."

He made the thumbs up signal that humans used instead of words. "You have a good night, then." He moved away from the door and returned to his companion.

"Are we going to the door?" Bramble asked.

Fernlight walked far enough away that the men would not see her. "You heard him, there is a camera. If they are looking, we can't just open the door and slip inside. He won't see us, but he will see the door move. Unless you have found a way to put a glamor on a door, or fool a recording."

"Not exactly," he said. "We need to get close to the door and I can stop the electricity to the camera for as long as we need."

Fernlight knew they had to get into the office. Going now meant they were more likely to have the time they needed. "Won't they be suspicious?"

"You mean because someone just asked about getting in, and the camera to the back entrance goes out, and the alarm gets a hiccup? You think they will look?" Bramble grinned as he asked the question.

"They will look. I know we will be invisible, and that we will be away from the door before they look, but we have to get out. They won't dismiss two problems with their protections. Would you?"

Bramble cackled. "I wouldn't have security that could be so

easily overcome. The humans still have a lot to learn about magic." He handed her more than half of the remaining spell. "If we don't stop Keenan, the Zeke, and this Talbot Ryce human, they will learn too quickly and not understand the consequences. We don't have to go out right away. We can wait until people start to arrive in the morning and then slip out."

"They will notice a fairy and a sprite leaving." Fernlight knew the invisibility would not last until morning. "And I don't want to spend any more time than necessary that far from the ground."

He patted her arm. "We will come to the main floor when we are done. I'm sure there are plenty of hiding places. I will have a glamor to make me human. Can't you disguise yourself too?"

Fernlight worried that being so far up in the air would deplete her energy. She straightened her shoulders and pushed away the doubts that were crowding her. "We'll worry about it when the time comes."

Taking the spell, she walked with Bramble back to the building. The guards didn't look up this time.

Chapter 30

Breaking in was as easy as it had been with Keenan and Zeke. With every successful attempt, Bramble seemed to get more proficient. This time there were no fried alarms.

The door led into a long corridor that ended with two doors. One said *employees only* and the other, very conveniently, *stairs*.

Bramble went to the second door. He moved his hands over it without touching the metal. "No alarms. Well, there are alarms, but they are not active. I wonder why? Do you think the humans walk all the way up this building? They would be very tired when they got to the top. Will you be able to walk up fifty floors? I can fly, don't worry about me."

Fernlight tried not to think about the number of stairs. "We have no choice." She reached around Bramble and turned the handle. A short flight of steps ended in another door. This one was unlabeled, but it had a small window in it.

Bramble reached it first. "An elevator! That makes sense! Lucky you, we don't have to walk." He pushed through the door and held it open for her.

There were two elevator doors and one button. Fernlight pressed it; it lit up.

"Wait!" Bramble rushed past her and flew to the top of the corner. He placed his hands on a black orb and then sighed. "They might have seen us. We have to be more careful. There are cameras everywhere." He came back to the ground and started pressing the button. "Come on! We need to get out of here."

Whether it was because of Bramble's insistent calling, or simply a coincidence, the elevator arrived before Fernlight could remind Bramble that they were invisible. He rushed inside, and frantically beckoned for her to join him.

"Do we know for sure that the cameras are fooled by the spell? As soon as I saw it, I started to get scared that the cameras would be able to see us." Bramble cowered in the corner of the elevator.

Fernlight reached across and pressed the button that would take them to the floor for Talbot Ryce's office. It had never occurred to her that the camera would not be fooled. "If the camera can see us anyway, then we are already caught. Since no one has come to stop us, I think we're safe. Are the cameras on all of the time?"

Her words seemed to give Bramble some reassurance. "I don't know. Perhaps I should research these things before we come out. I will try to do better next time." Bramble shook his wings out and seemed to regain his composure. "I guess we don't have to worry when we get off the elevator, because I will deal with a camera if it's there. If there's a computer, I could do some research really quickly, while we look around."

The elevator arrived at their floor with a *bing* that Fernlight hoped was not picked up by any listening devices. Bramble's reaction had her feeling paranoid, which might be a good thing if it sped up their search.

Bramble rushed across the hall to the large wooden doors

below a sign: RycePharma. There was another click, and Bramble grunted as he pushed the doors. Fernlight reached over him and added her strength. The doors were heavy and, with Bramble in the way, she couldn't quite hit the right point to make them swing easily. When they were open a foot, Bramble slipped inside, asking her to wait.

Fernlight felt exposed standing in the hallway even though it was deserted. It took a moment before Bramble stuck his head through the opening again and said it was clear to come in.

"I thought this would just be one small room," he said. "But it's huge, and there are many desks here, and there is another room across the way. I will open that door, but maybe you should be the one to search in there, and I will quickly look through all of these other desks. That way if someone comes, I will be able to run away."

And I will be trapped.

Fernlight didn't argue. They did not have time. She would be as quick as she could inside the office, and then she would be outside where she could also run away.

Inside, the room was clearly for a man with money and a desire to display his wealth. The desk was made from something like glass. There was a computer sitting on top. The chair was made of dead cows; humans called it leather. There were pictures on the walls, books on shelves, and awards arranged in a case. Fernlight saw that each one had the name Talbot Ryce. He had won them for inventions that she didn't understand.

She opened the lid to the computer, and the screen came up asking for a password. She felt a familiar frustration and didn't even try to guess what the password was. There were no drawers in the desk, or in the bookcase, or anywhere in the office. She stepped out to the larger room and called Bramble to try to get into the computer.

"There is nothing here. I have looked at everything. There

are no papers, there are only three or four computers, and I can't figure out the password. So I may not be able to open this one. But I will try."

Bramble typed a variety of letters and numbers into the password box, none of them accepted. Then the password box changed, and a message came up: *you are about to exceed your unsuccessful attempts.*

"See," Bramble said. "We will need more research to be done before we try this again. We should go. But first I need your phone. I am very worried about alarms. So I want to research before we leave."

Fernlight gave Bramble the phone. She wasn't sure how much he could find out in a short time, but now she was worried too.

Bramble pressed some keys, read what was on the screen, hit some other things, and then jerked in surprise. "The elevators might be in the control of the security guards. They might know someone came up here. We have to walk down the stairs. We can't take the chance that they will shut the elevators down on us."

Walking down would be a little easier than coming up would have been, Fernlight thought.

Chapter 31

Halfway down the stairs, Fernlight felt the power of the earth, faint but there. It was comforting. Her phone buzzed and she pulled it out of her pocket. Unable to run downstairs and answer the phone, she stood still on the first landing she came to.

"What is going on, why are you stopping?" Bramble whisper-shouted at her. "We still have to be invisible when we get out."

"It's Mamoru." Fernlight said, pressing the accept picture. "Hello?"

Bramble reached over her, pressed screen couple of times and suddenly Mamoru's voice was loud over the speaker. Fernlight almost dropped the phone. Bramble jabbed some buttons on the side, and volume went down.

"Are you there?"

"Yes. Bramble is here with me. We can't really talk right now. We have just searched the office."

"I am also in a somewhat perilous situation." Mamoru was whispering. "Will you be safe in ten minutes?"

Fernlight looked at Bramble, they had no guarantees. "Probably. Would you call us back?"

"It would be better if you called me, I need an excuse to leave here. I am not in a position to make phone calls repeatedly." The call ended.

Fernlight didn't waste time discussing it with Bramble. She held onto her phone and continued running down the stairs.

"There is a flaw in Heath's spell," Bramble said as he floated ahead of her.

Fernlight knew that the fairy was slowing down to keep her company. The least she could do was talk to him. "And what is that?"

Bramble threw up his hands as though she should have thought of it. "It should contain something that tells us that we are still invisible. This not knowing is very wearing on me."

The closer they got to the ground, the better Fernlight felt, and the faster she could move. At the bottom, they pushed through the only door, and found themselves in the elevator lobby.

"I wonder what time people start work here," Bramble said as he pressed his ear against the door to the stairs that led outside. "It would be much easier if one of the doors was open. But if there are people there, they are not speaking. Let me go first," Bramble said, a tremble starting in his wings. "I will be very brief. But I can fly away from them faster than you can run."

Fernlight did not want to be separated from her companion. Before she could say that, Bramble was through the door. Standing alone in the lobby, she became very aware of the camera. It was like a spirit watching her every move. Only spirits who were on the edge of turning to demons would watch someone like that.

The door swung open, and Bramble waved her through. "No one was there. I will disable the alarm again, and we must run to the door. If we are not invisible, we must go fast enough that they cannot catch us."

They would have to talk to Mamoru while standing on the street. It was not very private, but Fernlight had no choice. The only thing they could do was move as far away as possible from the building.

"It's not that far to Banks', maybe we should go there, and have some mead, and you could have a beer. And then we could be more calm. And then you could phone Mamoru and we would sound brave."

As much as she would've liked to sit in Banks' and chat with other Real Folk, Fernlight felt the time slipping through their fingers. "It is only a few hours until daybreak," she said. They approached the area where they had first seen Keenan. "We will talk to Mamoru. If there is nothing more we can do tonight, we will go to Banks' and I will buy you all the mead you want."

She led Bramble into a dark alley, checked the time, and made the call.

"I assume you are safe?" Mamoru said instead of hello.

"We are safe," Fernlight said. "We have not found anything, even though we searched his office."

"Are you sure that no one will know you were there? It is critical that we do not tip him off."

Bramble moved closer to the phone. "No one will know, because we were very careful, and I put the alarms to sleep. But we didn't find anything."

"It is not a surprise," Mamoru said. "I would be shocked to think this man would keep incriminating evidence like this in his office where it could be seen by accident."

A beer at Banks' was sounding better to Fernlight by the second. The case may be important, and inside she worried that it was too much for their first one. She felt that they took so few steps forward that failure was guaranteed.

"Where do we go next?" she asked. Her only idea was to return to Heath and see if he had healed. Now that they knew who the man was, they could ask Heath to track him.

"A man like Talbot Ryce is able to hide the details of his life very well. No one questions his need for secrecy; they call it privacy, but when it is not so innocent, it makes it very difficult to stop him."

Mamoru's voice was flat. He was keeping tight control on his feelings, so tight none came through. Fernlight wondered if he had admired Talbot Ryce before everything they learned.

"But if we can't find where he is, how are we going to stop him? Should we stop now? Are we all done?" Bramble was working himself up into a state again.

As Fernlight reached out to touch Bramble and calm him down, Mamoru started speaking again. "This ability to keep his private life private makes it difficult, but not impossible. Tonight, I was able to enter the chairman's office and search his files. I have Talbot Ryce's home address. The real one, not the one that he declares publicly because he is unable to hide behind privacy when he is on the board of such an institution as HOP-D."

"Will he be there?" Fernlight asked.

"It is possible, but unlikely. If he is indeed hiding himself, I believe he would have taken a suite in a hotel, or some other place. You must be careful when you search. What I am hoping you will find is some record of his drug use, or his current location. I cannot help but worry that without him in custody we lose control over the destiny of this drug."

"We are wasting time. Give us the address and we will search. If he is asleep, we can still search. If you don't tell us now, we will have to search in the daylight. And that is more dangerous."

Fernlight realized that Bramble's impatience came in handy sometimes. She chose not to add her voice to the conversation.

"I think you should take someone with you, one of my investigators. I have one I can trust."

Humans would only get in the way, Fernlight thought. And even if they didn't, they would interfere with Bramble's ability to work.

"We will be safe," Fernlight said. "I think it best that we leave your investigator until we need an official presence." It sounded very professional to her when she thought it, but perhaps a little petulant in delivery.

Mamoru was silent. The only reason that Fernlight knew the call was still in play was that the little picture on the screen remained green.

Is he going to waste the whole night?

"How do I know you will be safe?" Mamoru finally said.

"I thought the important thing was to catch this man and stop the spread of the drug," Bramble said. "If he succeeds, it will affect all people; Real Folk and humans. I am not willing to put my children and my wife at risk, and that means not worrying about being too safe and losing our opportunity."

Fernlight had never heard Bramble being so commanding. She sometimes forgot he was the king of his people.

"You will call me as soon as you're finished. I do not wish to be worried about you any longer than necessary. You are right. This is about the drug, but I do not wish for you to take unnecessary risks."

"We will not," Fernlight said.

It is up to us to determine what is unnecessary. "What is the address?"

Mamoru told him, and Bramble knew that it was far across the city from where they stood. For a human, if he was walking, it would take more than an hour. Even if he had a car, Bramble had noticed that cars often took a longer route because they had to be on special roads. For Real Folk, when they could find gardens to pass through it became easier. There were secret paths and tunnels that used the magic of the earth to speed their passage.

"The fastest way would be for us to go to the forest," Bramble said. "Do you think we can avoid seeing Beacon?" He was so tired he didn't even have to stop himself from talking more.

Fernlight tucked the phone into her pocket. "We can't take the chance. We only have an hour or two before the sun is up. Maybe even less, because there are no clouds. It won't matter if he's home, but if his neighbors are watching, there is no way for us to hide in the daylight. And we don't have time to get more invisibility spell."

"Let's go, there are a few paths we can take that don't link to the forest, but it's still going to mean we have to run. Well, you have to run; I can fly."

Chapter 32

Fernlight didn't slow him down that much, Bramble reflected as they stepped from the last path to face a large house. He wondered how many children Talbot Ryce had to need such a large home. And if he had children would they be awake and interrupt the search? And what would happen to them when Talbot Ryce was captured?

Fernlight pointed to the corner of the house. "We should use the hedges to get to that place. See the window? Maybe you can look and see if anybody is moving around."

Bramble didn't wait for Fernlight to follow him. He rushed to the side of the house, sliding through the Privet hedge with a quick hello to the head of the fairy household. He peeked in the window; there was a large room inside filled with furniture and lots of pretty things on tables and shelves. But nothing was out of place. It was very much like the office and it felt, even just looking at it, like the house was empty.

He saw Fernlight's reflection in the glass as she came up behind him. "Go around the side of the house and see if it's the same in another room. I don't think anybody is watching, all of the houses around here are dark."

Fernlight simply nodded and slid away like a shadow.

Bramble placed his ear against the wooden frame of the window. If anyone was inside, he might be able to hear their breathing. Fairies were well known for their ability to hear things other people couldn't. And he was the best of the fairies. He heard a creak, but it was only the house moving a little. There were no footsteps, there was no breathing.

Across the room he saw Fernlight pass the window. There was nothing more he could learn here. He moved back and followed her path to the other side of the house. When he arrived, she turned and said, "It all looks the same. It also doesn't smell like anyone has walked on the lawn for at least a few days."

Bramble trusted that a sprite would know if there was any damage to the grass. "How are we going to get in? I don't see any blinking lights on the doors, but if he is very rich and he has a secret, he would have alarms. And cameras, I haven't seen any of those either."

Fernlight moved a little farther along the side of the house, to where there was a door. "If there was an alarm, would we be able to tell from here?"

The door was wooden, but it had a window in it. Bramble knew from his experience that most alarms worked when something that should be together was taken apart. But all of that equipment would be inside. He moved to the far corner of the window and squished his face up against it to try to see the inside of the door, but it was the wrong angle. "I don't feel any electricity in the door, so if there is an alarm, it's very different from what I know." He looked around them. "The good news is that we can open the door, and if the alarm goes off, then we can run and hide in the gardens. Not like in the building, where there were no gardens for us to hide in. Shall I open the door? Are you ready to run?"

"If we have to hide, then I will go toward the trees in the

back of the lot. They're big enough that I could hide amongst them." She took a breath. "Go ahead and open the lock."

Bramble looked to where she pointed. There were four Chestnut trees there, old ones, very big ones. Fernlight could make herself invisible there. He hoped that the Privet fairy in residence would not object to a visit.

He reached out and sent his magic into the lock, he felt the insides move to unlock the door, but he also felt the drain on his own power.

Fernlight was the first one to enter, as soon as Bramble pushed the door open. He was relieved, because he was afraid of what would be there.

"It smells like no one is here," Fernlight said. "We still need to be fast. Do you want to search upstairs, or down here?"

Bramble glanced around, there only seemed to be four rooms on this floor. And they were all empty. And if he knew humans, the bedrooms would be upstairs. That's where the danger lay. "I will check here, and if I finish before you do, I will come upstairs and help you."

Fernlight simply walked away, as though she was as scared as Bramble of disturbing something.

The four rooms were not as simple to search as Bramble originally thought. The small room was a washroom, and it didn't take him long to find nothing. But the other rooms were full of exciting shiny objects. And there were so many cupboards, shelves, and drawers to explore that he didn't know where to start.

He flitted through each of the rooms; one a kitchen, one with chairs and a big table along with a big cabinet filled with pretty dishes and glasses. Under the cabinet were four drawers, all of them locked. He moved to the third room before starting his detailed search. This room had comfortable furniture, and a big screen on the wall. There were some cupboards, and a few unlocked drawers. He decided to start here because the kitchen was all cupboards and drawers.

He looked inside every hidden space, but all he found were books and magazines. None of them had any secret writing. Fernlight had not returned, so there must be some things to check upstairs. He decided to leave the kitchen for last, and went into the room with all the chairs. He didn't try to open the cabinet that contained all of the pretty china and glasses, because he could see every area through the glass doors. Each of the six drawers opened with a dribble of magic into the locks. Three of the drawers contained cloths, some big that would fit the table, and some small that matched the big ones. Bramble knew that if he pulled out a big one, he would not be able to fold it back up again. So he poked at each one, feeling for anything hard inside; there was nothing. Of the last three drawers, one contained nice forks and spoons, the second contained bigger spoons, bigger forks and two really big knives, and the third was empty.

In the kitchen, all of the drawers and cupboards were unlocked. They contained pots and pans and more plates. One or two had food in cans and boxes. And there were three jars of honey in the last one.

Fernlight still had not come downstairs. Bramble could feel the tension stirring in his heart. His wings trembled a little. He would have to go upstairs. If there were humans up there, perhaps they had Fernlight held captive. He couldn't call out, because if they were asleep he didn't want to wake them. And even though the house smelled empty. Humans were tricky.

Chapter 33

He flew as slowly as he could to the bottom of the stairs, taking the time to try to calm his nerves. He could see that the stairs turned about halfway up. What he couldn't see was at the top half of the stairs. His wings trembled more, and he was afraid that he would lose control of them. He allowed himself to float down to the floor, took a hold of the banister, and started to walk up the stairs. As he approached the turn, another creak sounded. Bramble couldn't breathe. *You can't be too scared; you have to be brave. If Fernlight is in trouble, you need to save her.*

The words didn't really help, he was still frozen to the carpet.

Another creak!

"Bramble?" The voice was quiet, but it was Fernlight.

Bramble realized he had his eyes closed. He opened them to see his partner standing on the step in front of him looking at him with a puzzled expression. He didn't know what to say to make himself look less foolish. "Did you find anything?" The rest of the words were swallowed up in his embarrassment.

"Nothing. You?" Fernlight pointed towards the bottom of the stairs.

Bramble found himself able to move, and he backed down the stairs. "Nothing. Well, there was something, but I don't think it has anything to do with the case. But I am running low on honey. And there are jars in the kitchen. And I was wondering if it would be okay if you opened one and refilled my supply."

"A little can't hurt," Fernlight said. "Show me where you found it."

As they turned to go back to the kitchen, heavy footsteps sounded on the front steps. Bramble's wings started fluttering again and he had to breathe slowly to keep from fainting. A clang and then letters spilled through the opening in the door. The mail arrived. Bramble couldn't bring himself to reach for it. He was too occupied with calming down.

Fernlight gathered the envelopes and magazines. "Nothing that will help," she said. "Junk mail, magazines and some bills."

Bramble took in a deep breath. This human world was filled with interruptions. "Can we get the honey now?" His voice was tiny even in his own ears.

"Sure—"

The doorbell rang. This time Bramble had no warning. The world got grey and he felt cold.

"Don't panic," Fernlight hissed. "I need you with me."

They both stood like stones. Then a card came through the mail slot and Bramble heard footsteps retreat.

Fernlight looked at the card as she scattered the other mail. "He has a parcel to pick up. Do you think we should try to intercept it?"

"No! We have to finish searching. He wouldn't have the drug sent through the mail, he wouldn't take the chance, right?"

Fernlight straightened and headed to the kitchen. "I guess. Now, where was the honey?"

Bramble wondered why Talbot Ryce wasn't here. "We aren't getting anywhere, how can this man not have anything in his office or his home? He is somewhere. And it is where the Zeke can take his drugs."

"We haven't checked the basement yet," Fernlight said as she screwed the lid back on the honey and placed it in the cupboard.

"I didn't see any way to get there. I opened all the doors, but none led downstairs. But as we passed the house, I noticed there were windows, but they all had curtains drawn so I couldn't see what was in there."

Fernlight moved around the kitchen pressing on the walls. Bramble watched, but she found nothing. Then she moved into the short corridor between the kitchen and the room with the chairs and table. When she pressed on the left wall, Bramble heard a click.

"Another hidden door? Humans are very tricky. I must always check for secret doors. Can you see anything down there?"

Fernlight stepped aside enough for Bramble to look for himself. The stairs ended and opened up into a wide space. She carefully stepped down, Bramble close behind her. He was willing to be brave, but Fernlight was bigger, and was more able to take a scary surprise.

They stood at the bottom of the stairs looking around. It was one large room. At one end was a desk, with a computer on it. At the other end was another big screen on the wall and comfortable chairs, and a big glass cabinet filled with bottles and glasses.

"I will check the computer," Bramble said. "Maybe this one will have less security on it. And I can find his password."

Fernlight walked around the room, while Bramble tried to

enter the password on the computer. It was just like at the office. He couldn't guess the password, and then he was told that he would run out of tries.

"Bramble? Come look at this."

He looked up to see Fernlight standing in front of a picture. Bramble closed the laptop and joined her. In the picture Talbot Ryce was in a forest, and behind him there was a wooden building, and hanging from his fingers were hooks that were lodged in the mouths of two large fish. "Do you think this is where he is? How are we going to find it? It looks very remote. It would be a perfect place to hide."

Fernlight looked around and then pointed at a cabinet in the corner. "Maybe he has papers in that cabinet."

Bramble flitted over to the filing cabinet and sent a little power into the frame. There was a lock, but it was not engaged. "Maybe we should phone Mamoru, and tell him what we saw, and maybe he can find a record of that place."

Fernlight didn't answer. Bramble turned around to see her staring intently at the picture. He flitted over to her and tried to see what she was looking for. "Does it have a label on it?" Bramble reached up to take the picture from the wall. "Maybe on the back he wrote the address. That will save us a lot of time. Or if not the address, a clue. It would be better if we didn't have to call Mamoru, because he'll tell us not to do it. For someone who wants us to solve this case, he keeps trying to get in our way."

Fernlight held him back from touching the frame. "You're right about all of that, but I don't want to move the picture just yet. Let me look at all the details. And then I will turn it over. I'm afraid that if we move it too quickly, we'll leave a mark."

Bramble stared at the picture with her. He hoped that they would be able to commit it to memory, but what if it was just like his picture, and it disappeared?

Chapter 34

"Do you have paper with you?" Fernlight asked. Between Bramble and herself, they should be able to remember all of the details in the picture. And, if they had a drawing, they would have something they could hand to Mamoru if necessary.

Bramble turned away from the photograph. "No. Why don't you take a picture of it on your phone? We don't need to draw everything. If you take a picture, you could check it and if it's not good enough, you could take another picture. And a picture on your phone can be sent to Mamoru if we need to."

Fernlight pulled out her phone and tapped it to bring it alive. There were lots of pictures humans called icons on the screen, and one really did look like a tiny camera. She tapped it and was about to ask Bramble how to take a picture and she realized it was very clear. The first picture she took wasn't very good, there was too much glare from the glass of the frame. Bramble standing over her made it difficult to concentrate. "Do you want to go back to the files? I can ask if I need any help."

"Oh yeah, the files. I'll let you know if I find anything. And we could take a picture of anything we find. We should be taking a lot more pictures. Why didn't I think of it earlier?"

Fernlight smiled, it felt good to know that she was not the only one having difficulty understanding how human technology could help them. Perhaps there was something to being reliant on only one way of doing things. For Real Folk, it was magic, and for humans it was technology.

She heard a click and turned to see Bramble opening the first file drawer. Knowing he would call her if he found anything, or if he had any questions, she concentrated on getting a good picture of the cabin. When that was done, she carefully lifted the picture from the wall, but there was nothing on the back.

The cabinet would only open one drawer at a time, so she lurked behind Bramble as he flicked quickly through each file. There wasn't much in there, maybe ten folders. The same was true for the next drawer, and the next. But there was nothing that Bramble thought would help them. Fernlight wasn't sure what they were looking for, Bramble was the one who had a talent for simply looking and finding what he needed.

"This might be it, but I don't know how to read it. And it's very big." Bramble spread a sheet of paper on the desk.

Fernlight looked at it, took out her camera, and tried to get it in one shot, but it wouldn't fit. "I will have to take several pictures; can you make them all come together?"

Bramble shrugged. "We'll see, but we can also send all of these pictures to Mamoru if we have to. It's too bad Heath doesn't have any magic. If he did, we could send him the pictures, and he might be able to cast a spell on them. But I don't know if a picture of something carries the same magical properties as the original. Heath might know."

As Bramble chattered on, Fernlight took four pictures of the piece of paper, trying to overlap in case they had to print and stick the individual shots together.

"I think we should leave," Fernlight said closing the camera on her phone. "There's nothing else here, unless you have another idea. If we go back to the office, we could use the computer at least."

"Was there anything upstairs? That's the only place I didn't go. The first floor doesn't contain anything for us." Bramble replaced the paper and pressed the top of the filing cabinet as he spoke. A quiet click told Fernlight that the doors were locked again.

"A bedroom, that had nothing but the bed. A room with exercise equipment, and two other rooms which were empty."

"Only one bedroom? For only one man? He has this big house, and this cabin, wherever that is, and it's just him?"

"Humans are different from us in many ways." Fernlight wondered if they needed to do more research on humans. It seemed to her that there were many varieties.

"Everything looks the same as when we came down, this is a good time to leave. We should go back to the office; you are right about that. But we should phone Mamoru. We don't know what that paper was about, I just have a really strong feeling it will help. Mamoru will maybe know; it's a human thing, and maybe it takes a human to understand."

Fernlight took one more look around, feeling sure that if Talbot Ryce returned he wouldn't see anything out of place. Bramble was right; it didn't look like they'd been there. They left the room and stepped through the secret door to the hallway between the kitchen and the other rooms.

"Mr. Ryce? Are you back from the cabin?"

Fernlight froze. Bramble pressed himself against her back, his trembling feeling like it was coming from her own body. She could only hope he would take comfort from the contact. There was no way they could speak. The human woman in the kitchen was too close.

Fernlight could hear her walking around, but the footsteps

were not approaching. She backed carefully into the other room, but there was nowhere to hide there. They couldn't go upstairs; they would be trapped. They couldn't go downstairs, that was also a trap. She could see the front door. Would they be able to get it open? Was Bramble in good enough shape to disable any alarms? The thought reminded her that the human woman would not have been able to enter without setting off the alarm, so it must be turned off.

It would be better to leave by the back door, where they could be within the trees and hedges before the woman noticed.

As these thoughts were going through Fernlight's mind, Bramble remained close to her, his fear appeared to be diminishing with a little distance from the human.

She moved to the furthest point away from the kitchen and chanced a whisper. "Can we get to the kitchen?"

Bramble nodded and pointed across the room.

Fernlight saw the staircase, and beyond that a side corridor, just before the opening to the other room. They needed to know where the woman was. If that corridor led to the kitchen, and the woman wasn't looking, they might be safe.

It would've been better if Bramble were the one to take a peek, but Fernlight didn't think he was in any state to do that. She motioned him to stay in the corner. Choosing her steps carefully, she made her way to the staircase, and stood there listening intently for evidence of where the human was.

All Fernlight could tell was that she was in the kitchen. If she came out in this direction, Fernlight would be caught. She crept back to join Bramble. "Can you make her go? At least out of the kitchen, we only need a moment."

Bramble pulled out the contents of his bag. This was when they needed the invisibility spell. Real Folk magic could not make a human do anything against their will; only the powerful spirits that controlled life and death could do so. That didn't mean subtle spell work was needed either. The woman was already curious about Talbot Ryce being home, so she knew that perhaps someone was here. But she didn't feel threatened, because she continued to bustle about the kitchen.

Bramble laid out the sachets of spells on the floor. He leaned in and spoke directly in her ear. "I don't think I have anything that will help. I could make her sneeze, but she might see us, the rest of the spells are more about holding power, than they are about changing minds."

Fernlight saw a spell that might work. "You can call a spider."

Bramble grinned. "Yes! I could call him to the other side of the kitchen, and she would run there because I would call a big one, and we could leave. Then, before she even knows we're gone, I will call the spider back. We do not wish to make them angry with us. They will blame me if she kills him."

Bramble cast the spell, and nothing happened.

"Maybe another spell will work," Fernlight said, disappointed.

Bramble started creeping towards the staircase. He turned and beckoned her to join him. "It takes time."

Almost as soon as he finished speaking, the human woman screamed and started speaking in another language. Fernlight hazarded a look around the corner to find her holding a paper towel and running towards the far counter. Bramble opened the door, and they both slipped out.

As they ran for the trees, Bramble said, "I was very brave, wasn't I?"

Chapter 35

They'd arrived back in the office exhausted. There was nothing they could do after they sent Mamoru the information but wait. He'd acknowledged receipt immediately, but after two hours with no response, Fernlight decided they needed to rest. Bramble had excitedly run off to meet with his wife, promising to return with enough energy now that he knew how much they needed, and a wider range of spells.

Fernlight had been more reluctant to recharge her energy. Standing in the dirt under a tree in a park when people were around was bound to bring stares. But she still couldn't risk going into the forest, where Beacon would assign her tasks. Thankfully, Bella had seen her with her feet in the earth, and spent some time chatting. The way her neighbor accepted Fernlight restored her feeling that humans were not all evil.

By the time Mamoru called with the location of the cabin, they were both feeling anxious. She hoped that her emotions were not as visible as Bramble's.

Now they stood in the shade of the old trees, on the side of a mountain, looking down on the cabin in the picture. It'd taken hours to travel on magical paths from the city to this location. "He's here," she said, pointing to the car parked just outside.

"How are we going to find the drug if he is here? Are we going to try and arrest him? Can we arrest him? Maybe we should have said yes to Mamoru when he offered to come." Bramble's voice was creeping up into the non-hearing range.

"We need to see what he's doing," Fernlight said. "We do not want to catch him, that is for Mamoru to do. Remember he said he would drive towards the cabin and wait for us near-by." It suddenly didn't seem like such a good idea that the only person with authority was not standing right beside them. But Mamoru couldn't work the way they did, and she did not want to explain every move they made.

"Maybe he is not inside," Bramble said, a note of hope in his voice. "I mean that's his car, I assume, but that doesn't mean he's inside. Maybe he's gone for a walk."

Fernlight thought it was more likely that Talbot Ryce was inside the cabin, or not very far away. He came here so that his transition was private. When Zeke had a new batch of the drug, it would only be a matter of an hour or so before it was in Talbot Ryce's hands. And that container had seemed mostly ready to her. For all they knew Talbot Ryce had completed his transformation and was simply biding his time until the confer-ence tomorrow night.

"We need to know," she said. "You wait here, if I am caught you must find Mamoru."

Bramble's grasp on the thin branch of the young tree beside them was so tight the tree trembled. "But I can fly close and be gone fast, and you must walk. We are all very fast, but remember he is half magic already."

She appreciated the fact that Bramble would not let his fear easily hold him back. But he would be faster finding Mamoru if everything went wrong. "If we had invisibility spells, that would make sense. But I am a sprite and I will be almost invisible as long as I stay within the trees. He has not cleared anything but the undergrowth, so I can almost get to the window without leaving cover."

She didn't wait for an answer, simply blended in with the surrounding trees and moved towards the cabin. There were windows on the side, and in the front. The building was very small. It was possible that she would be able to see the whole interior from any window.

As she approached, she listened closely, but there were no sounds. If Talbot Ryce were inside, and trying his magic, or even undergoing the transformation, surely she would hear something.

The trees closer to the cabin were not well. Fernlight touched two and sank her senses into their trunks. Someone had been pulling their energy. That was not something a sprite would do. You pull energy from the earth, use it, or provide it to the plants around you. And now that she thought about it, where were the sprites of this forest?

There could be no answer to that question, so she crept closer to the cabin. Placing her body against the wooden logs of the wall, she carefully peered through the window. There were two rooms walled off inside, but the rest of the cabin was visible. On the table in the center of the room was the jar of blue liquid that they had seen in Zeke's lab. Or if not that jar, another identical to it. If Mamoru was correct, and this potion was to be injected, surely there was enough in that container to transform hundreds of people.

That was worrying enough, but there were scorch marks on the walls and floor. The cabin, now that she was this close, reeked of magic gone wrong. The only thing that didn't scare her was that Talbot Ryce was not here. She circled the building, checking both of the walled-out rooms, and no one was there. The bedroom was definitely being inhabited.

. . .

FROM HIS POSITION in the trees, Bramble still felt like he was being watched. He kept looking up and around, but only for a second because it was important he watch Fernlight. But there was no one out there. Talbot Ryce was not watching him.

When Fernlight moved around the building out of his sight, Bramble wanted to rush forward and make sure she was not walking into danger. But before he could raise his courage, she returned to the back, and started moving toward him.

"Why are you here? This is not Bramble territory." A Laurel fairy was looking down from a low branch of a tree.

Bramble squeezed the twig he was holding onto, hoping that his sudden fright had not been apparent to this woodland fairy. He was a king even if this wasn't Bramble territory. He swallowed the lump in his throat, and looked at the other fairy with what he hoped was a scornful glance. "We are here to save the world."

"Well that is very important, but I need to tell my queen about all intruders. Human, like the man in that cabin, or Real Folk."

"What do you know about the man in the cabin? Do you know where he is? Do you know what he's been doing?" On the last question, Bramble remembered his manners. "Pay my respects to your queen, please. When we have saved the world, I will come and visit with her. My wife will be happy to visit this area." Bramble knew full well his wife would not want to come out here. She enjoyed being able to get close to the forest in the city. There she could talk to important sprites and high rank fairies, so she could get the latest gossip. This was too isolated.

"Why should I answer your questions?"

"Because your queen would be very angry with you if you allow that man to continue what he is doing," Fernlight said as she stepped close to them.

The Laurel fairy looked up at Fernlight, righting himself on the branch to take in her full height. "Is that why all of the sprites left?"

Bramble wondered why he was determined not to be helpful. Perhaps it was to do with the isolation here.

Fernlight looked around her. "No, and I would like to know where they are. I will certainly be looking into that. It must be difficult for you, when no one is helping you to keep the plants healthy."

Bramble watched the Laurel fairy warm under concerns about his hard life.

"Yes. We work very hard, but fairies are not responsible for trees. We only do what we can for them, so they help to keep our Laurel bushes lush." He looked down at Bramble and then back at Fernlight. "The man is at the river. It is a long walk for a human."

"Do you think that you could warn us when he starts to come back?" Fernlight asked. "We will be inside his house, looking for a way to stop him from being so dangerous."

The Laurel fairy puffed up as though the task had made him more important. "I told the queen he was dangerous. I saw him pulling energy from the trees near the house. That is not what humans do. He was acting very much like a Real Folk, and if the world is changing that much, it will not be good for fairies. I will do as you ask."

Bramble watched the Laurel fairy run back into the trees. "How did you make him so cooperative? He should have answered my questions, I am a king even though I'm not his king, he should respect me."

Fernlight chuckled and beckoned him towards the house. She seemed more relaxed now that they knew they would not be caught. "I made him feel important. You made him feel like you expected him to obey."

Bramble considered her words as they approached the cabin. If he was simply a fairy, living within the world of Bramble fairies, he would be right. Royalty would always be respected, no matter the tribe. It seemed that to be an investigator, and to achieve his goal, he would need to learn more than just how to find things in the Internet.

The cabin wasn't even locked. Bramble was glad he did not have to expend energy on releasing the security. He had more fairy treasure, but he would prefer to save it for when he needed it for more important things.

Inside the cabin, Fernlight started poking through things that were sitting on the table and counter and floor. Bramble stood still waiting for the feeling of dread to pass, but it didn't. "Bad magic. He has been doing bad magic. Very dangerous, even for Real Folk."

The contents of the jar called to him again, but Bramble forced himself to ignore it. It was clear from what he saw on the table that Talbot Ryce was trying to make spells. There were pieces of herbs, scraps of twigs and bark, and a few small pots of liquid; one of them was blood.

"This is too easy."

Bramble looked up from the table at Fernlight's words. She held the notebook in her hand. It was open and she was tracing some words with her fingers. Bramble flew over to look over her shoulder.

I can tell my transformation is almost complete. The switching between reality and unreality seldom happens today, and I was able to summon an image.

I do not have time to test my theory here. I must return home and gather some of those magical creatures to test. If my assumptions are correct, their death will release their magic into my body.

Bramble stopped breathing.

Chapter 36

Fernlight stared at the words on the page in front of her. She could hear Bramble muttering in the corner where he had fallen when he'd read the words over her shoulder. How would they be able to save all of the Real Folk?

The door banged open against the wall. Fernlight snapped the book closed as she looked up. There was Talbot Ryce standing in the doorway, his hand gripping the Laurel fairy's arm.

"Put that back! Move away from the table." The man's voice crackled with power.

Fernlight did what she was told. Not because his power was such that it compelled her, but to keep his focus on her. If he had not seen Bramble yet, that would be an advantage.

"This one said you had another fairy with you," Talbot Ryce said, shaking the Laurel fairy.

Fernlight stared at the Laurel fairy, hoping he would not contradict her. "He left. He's gone to get the authorities."

The Laurel fairy's eyes were wide, but it seemed like his fear did not stop him from realizing that it would be better for them all if Bramble remained hidden.

Talbot turned and slammed the door closed behind him. "Well then, we must hurry with what I have to do. There are only two of you, but I hope that this will be a test of my theory." He nodded at the book. "I assume you read it?"

Fernlight had to concentrate on the words. Talbot Ryce was more stable, but he still had not made the full transition. The crackling in his voice was like static, and it became louder when his body shifted. "Our magic doesn't work that way."

"Mine might. And there is no point in trying to stall until the authorities arrive. They cannot get in here while I am working. I purchased wards from a wizard before this started."

She knew that waiting for Mamoru to decide they were in trouble wouldn't work. But she could use the stall tactic to allow her to think of a way out.

Talbot shoved the Laurel fairy toward the table. Fernlight could see an eagerness in the man's eyes, and that emotions seemed to increase the flickering.

"It could also kill you. It is dangerous to test things with magic that is well known. It is suicide to do it with unknown magic."

He laughed at her words. "You see how I am. I cannot stay in this state. I must either complete the process, or I might as well die. I cannot run my business. I cannot lead anyone, let alone take over the world."

"How much of this drug have you taken?" If she could get any more information about the drug, Fernlight would take the risk. And the longer she could hold onto life for both her and the Laurel fairy, the longer she had to save them.

She couldn't remember what spells Bramble had brought back with him from his home. And she couldn't even figure out a way to prompt him to look. Without seeing how calm he was, Fernlight couldn't rely on Bramble taking any hints, or even being conscious.

"What does it matter?" Talbot Ryce asked. "You've never

seen that drug before. He assured me that it was unique." A frown crossed his face and his body flickered in and out. "He told me there was no one else using it. But he's a drug dealer, how can I be sure he didn't lie? Of course, I will have to kill him."

Talbot Ryce did not seem to be in a hurry to kill either the Laurel fairy or her. Fernlight waited while he tied the fairy to the leg of the table. He did it while keeping his gaze on her the entire time.

"Now you," Talbot Ryce said, beckoning her toward the table.

Fernlight didn't move.

"So, you still have some will of your own? Well, magic isn't the only thing that can make you obey." He backed to the low sofa that faced the window, reached between the cushions, and pulled out a gun. "It will work just as well if I shoot you where you stand. I just have to make a few preparations."

BRAMBLE WISHED that Fernlight was a fairy. Then they could talk without the human hearing them. The Laurel fairy had already told him how he'd been captured. He was spying on Talbot Ryce when the man suddenly turned and commanded him to reveal himself. Somehow Fernlight wasn't affected by the command. Maybe it was because she was so big, and her magic ran deep as the earth.

Without talking to her, he couldn't explain how he was going to rescue her. He hoped she could continue to talk to the man so that he wouldn't start casting his spells.

Bramble didn't have an invisibility spell — he never seemed to have one when he needed it — so he couldn't wander around the cabin creeping up on the man. But he could move fast. And the man? Maybe not. At least he wasn't now, but if he finished his spell who knew what would happen.

There was nothing within reach for Bramble to use as a weapon. And now the man had a gun. He couldn't wait too long, because every moment that went by everything got worse. And at some point, it would be beyond any fairy's ability to make right.

If he could get Fernlight free, then they could rescue the Laurel fairy. After they dealt with Talbot Ryce, of course.

Bramble called out to the Laurel fairy, using the high ranges of his voice. "I will rescue you. But first I need to get the sprite."

The Laurel fairy was trembling; he opened his mouth, but no sound came out. Bramble knew that feeling.

"Do you think you can bite him?"

The Laurel fairy shook his head.

"What is that damn squeaking?"

The human could hear them. Maybe not hear what he was saying, but he could hear that they were talking. There was no time left. If he waited, he would be found.

Bramble felt the fury building inside him. This man was going to kill them all. His wings stiffened and he launched himself at Talbot Ryce's face. Scratching and biting. The human dropped the gun and tried to swat him away, but Bramble was too fast. If he could keep fighting, then he would do enough damage to the man that maybe Fernlight could finish the job.

"Get away from me!" Talbot Ryce used the command voice. Bramble had no choice but to leave the fight. He rushed to the door and tried to open it, because the man had not told him where to go. But the door would not move.

"Stop! Don't—" next was a sound of pain.

Bramble turned to see Fernlight standing over the man, her fist still clenched. Talbot Ryce wasn't moving.

"Did you kill him? Are we safe?" Bramble asked as he flew toward the body.

As he arrived, the body flickered once and he saw the human's chest rise with a breath.

"No. And he won't stay down for long." Fernlight moved to the table and untied the Laurel fairy as she spoke.

"Where's the gun? You could shoot him." Bramble looked around. He'd heard the gun drop, but it was nowhere to be seen.

"He fell on it," Fernlight said. She passed Bramble and walked to the door, wrenching it open with just her strength. Bramble noticed a few sparks of a broken spell floating into the air. "I'm not going to move him and risk being caught again. We need to go."

Bramble knew that he would not be able to lift the gun. Even if he could, he would not be able to shoot it. Those things pushed back at you when they shot.

"Bramble, come on," Fernlight called. "We have to go. Look, he's recovering."

Bramble could see that Talbot Ryce's breathing was getting stronger. He looked around, but there was no sign of the Laurel fairy. And without any other suggestions, he had to follow Fernlight's lead. But first he picked up a knife from the table, probably the one Talbot Ryce would have used to kill them, and flew out to stab the car tires.

Outside they did not have to go more than ten steps before they found the entrance to the magical path. Bramble heard Talbot Ryce groaning as they sank into the path.

Chapter 37

Fernlight locked the office door behind Bramble. They were both exhausted from the rush back. Even if Talbot Ryce had been able to get to his vehicle right away, and fix his tires himself, he would still be traveling from the cabin. The only pause had been to let Mamoru know to meet them in the office.

"I need only a few minutes with my treasure," Bramble said. "It seems that every time we think we know how much power we need, the case gets harder. We need to think of a way to recharge fast. I can wait here for Mamoru if you want to go to the park."

Fernlight didn't waste energy on talking. She ran to the park and sank her feet into the soil. Maybe Heath would have a solution to their power needs. It sounded just like the kind of efficiency he would like. In the meantime, she would arrange for a large planter to be placed in their parking spot. It wasn't ideal, but there would be some energy in the soil.

When she returned, Bramble was still alone. A small relief. If Mamoru hadn't arrived yet, then Talbot Ryce must still be on the road.

"He said he was going to kill us," Bramble said. "He wants to kill lots of us, maybe all of us. That way he will have the only magic in the world."

Fernlight shuddered as she remembered the gleam in Talbot's eyes as he anticipated just the test of his theory. "Arianrhod will not let him," she said. The elemental who controlled the balance between life and death would protect them, or at least some of them. Fernlight wished she had the power to call to Arianrhod, but even the powerful druids had to wait on her wishes. It would be nice to know that she was watching.

"He's here," Bramble said, dragging Fernlight out of her thoughts. "Mamoru is here. We have to tell him now. This must be enough proof."

Fernlight open the door for Mamoru. The man looked harried, not his usual calm and stern demeanor. She wasn't sure whether she felt comforted or worried by the fact that the danger had an effect on him.

"I fear it might be time to end your involvement. For your own safety, of course." Mamoru sat in the client chair and took out his notebook. "You must tell me everything that happened."

"Everything that happened was this: we saw Talbot Ryce, and he tried to kill us. And he's planning to kill more of us. He wants our magic to be absorbed into him."

Fernlight touched Bramble's arm, knowing that the report had to be more detailed than that. "When we arrived at the cabin, we scouted around and saw it was empty. A local fairy confirmed where he was and promised to warn us if he started to come back to the cabin." She wondered if the Laurel fairy had stopped shaking long enough to report to his queen. "We searched inside and found his notebook. He seems to believe that to complete the transformation he needs the death of Real Folk. When we die, our magic returns to the world. Talbot

Ryce seems to think he can interrupt that process. He wanted to test it on us. We attacked him and managed to escape." She found it hard to get into any further details, not because she couldn't remember, but because her fear was still intense.

"Is it possible that he's right?" Mamoru didn't look at her; he was busy writing in the notebook.

"We don't know, but we can ask our wizard friend. Whether it works or not though, we do need to stop him. Because he will still kill Real Folk to test it."

Mamoru finished writing in his book, closed it and looked at Fernlight then at Bramble. "It is too dangerous for you to continue. I will take it from here."

"But HOP-D will not try to save us. Your organization will probably be on Talbot Ryce's side. Not to take over the world, maybe, but to take the magic." Bramble started flitting around the office.

Fernlight knew that Mamoru would try to argue. She also knew Bramble sounded afraid for good reason; after all, Mamoru worked for the organization. The truth was that she shared Bramble's fears.

"I don't agree, but I understand how you feel. I must clarify; I mean *I* need to handle this. This man can manipulate the people in my office. He is still on the board of HOP-D." He seemed to struggle for words. "I need to kill this man. I am sorry if that is too blunt."

Bramble stopped flitting and returned to stand in front of Mamoru. He looked up into the man's eyes, his body still, his wings relaxed. "You would do that for us? But isn't that a crime? I didn't think that you would be willing to do that."

Fernlight interrupted before Mamoru could answer. This had gone too far. "Yes, he is dangerous, but killing him won't end it. Are you willing to kill Keenan too? Or Zeke? And Talbot Ryce said that he suspects other men are taking this drug. Perhaps not just men, perhaps women too. We need to end all of it, and that means we need to find everyone and expose them. If they need to be killed, it will be after we have found all of the answers."

Mamoru looked at her, opened his mouth to answer, and then closed it again. He rubbed his brow with his hand. "I do not wish to kill anyone. I carry enough pain from before. I did not know other people were possibly taking the drug. You are right, we need all of our answers. But in the end, it cannot be you who kills a human."

Bramble looked at Fernlight, and she could almost hear him asking his questions.

"We cannot guarantee that," she said. "I hope that you will be able to deal with any consequences if we do. But we cannot chance this spreading. If you are not there when it needs to be done, I will do it. But I also hope it does not need to be done."

"I never thought that I would become judge and executioner," Mamoru said quietly. "I always vowed that I would allow judgment and punishment to be the field of others. My job was to bring the right person into that system. And now, here we sit, and I learn that sometimes a moral imperative is stronger than the law."

Bramble reached and touched Mamoru's shoulder. "We will try to make it so you can bring him to justice. I know why you don't want us to kill him. The humans are afraid that we will kill them already. But we cannot let this continue. *I* cannot let this continue."

Mamoru smiled at Bramble, and then stood. "I have work to do. I will try to find information on these other suspects. I imagine they will be attending Ryce's event, but from what you say, it will be to sabotage, or steal the magic, rather than to support him." He checked his watch. "You must rest, you are almost transparent, Bramble. And Fernlight, you are shrinking, if I am not mistaken."

Bramble turned to look at her. "Yes, you are six inches too short."

The events of the last day had drained them more than Fernlight noticed. Real Folk were rarely under the amount of stress that this case exposed them to. That, and the physical effort, was making it hard to hang onto energy. Fernlight locked the door behind Mamoru so they could set wards.

Chapter 38

Bramble woke from his nap. It had been refreshing to curl around his fairy treasure and allow the magic to seep back into his bones. Fernlight was sitting at her desk tapping on the keyboard. She was still shorter, but not quite as much as before.

"What are you looking for? Can I help? Are you feeling better? Have we heard from Mamoru?"

Fernlight looked up from the screen. "I have only been back for a few minutes. I am trying to find the list of attendees for the event this evening. If things go badly, and we need to confront him at the event, it would be better not to be surprised." She printed a list of names. "I'm finished, so no need for your help, thank you. I am feeling better, and Mamoru has not contacted us."

Bramble brought the printout to the desk. "Do you know any of these names? Maybe these people are also taking the drug? Not all of them, but some."

The phone rang and Bramble hoped it was Mamoru, so he answered it rather than waiting for Fernlight to speak.

It was Heath. "Is your magic back? Do you have the cure? Oh, let me put you on speaker."

"My magic is coming back, but it's not very reliable so I won't be doing any spells or creating any charms until it is. The good news is I'm not craving the drug, so for us it's not addictive. I can't speak for humans."

"We have lots of ideas for spells for you in the future. But that'll have to wait until we solve the case." Bramble stopped speaking and waited for Heath to tell them more. Maybe he did have a cure.

"I don't have the cure yet. I'm sorry, I couldn't work on it while my magic was gone. And now the way it is, even if I found the cure, we couldn't know for sure that it would work."

Bramble hoped that soon they would learn something that didn't give them more questions. And something that would stop Talbot Ryce. It would be nice to cure him, but maybe that wouldn't happen.

Fernlight leaned towards the phone, even though Bramble had told her several times that she could just talk, she seemed to think that she needed to be close to the phone.

"We are running out of time, Heath. Is there any way you would have a cure in the next few hours?" she asked.

"It doesn't work that way," he said. "It's not a progressive, almost there kind of thing. When I have the cure, you will have it. But I won't know from one second to the next if an experiment will work. I need to go away from the familiar, so I can focus only on this task."

"But it will be all over by the time you come back! If you don't have a cure by tonight, we might all be dead! Tomorrow, humans and Real Folk will all be gone or enslaved." Bramble's heart had started beating fast again. He closed his lips so he wouldn't make it worse. Fernlight would have to continue asking questions. At least for a little while.

"It doesn't matter," Heath said. "I can't speed up the process. And without more of the potion, there are some tests I cannot do. Can you get me more?"

Bramble looked at Fernlight. Maybe they could steal more from the Zeke.

"I don't think so," Fernlight said. "The jar that we took the first sample from is in the hands of the user."

"You know who he is?"

"His name is Talbot Ryce," Fernlight said. "But do not try to contact him. Heath, he is very dangerous."

There was a long pause. Bramble fidgeted, because he didn't know what to say. Fernlight seemed to know what Heath was thinking part of the time.

"It would help, but don't worry. You go about catching the bad guy, and I'll figure out how to cure him. I'll call you as soon as I know anything. But you won't be able to get in touch with me, I need isolation." Heath ended the call.

Bramble stared at the phone, then looked up at Fernlight. "He didn't even say goodbye. We could have told him more things; he didn't even want to hear about the way Talbot Ryce thinks he can finish the spell. We should call him back."

Fernlight nodded and pressed the button to call back. The line was busy.

Bramble was tired of waiting. They only had a handful of hours left to stop the event, and end Talbot's Ryce's plans. He could see that Fernlight felt the same way.

"We don't even know if he's back," she said. "But I'd be very surprised if he wasn't. He could be catching Real Folk right now and killing them."

Bramble looked up from where he was hunched over the computer keyboard. "But we have to wait for Mamoru. He said he would help us. If we're not here, how will he help us? And I don't like it when you act like this, I'm the one who was supposed to be impulsive."

Fernlight smiled. Bramble knew he could always make that happen, no matter how annoyed she was.

The office door opened. Bramble looked up and squealed in terror.

Standing inside the office, looking thinner and older than the last time they'd seen him, was Zeke Middleton.

Chapter 39

"What can we do for you?" Fernlight asked, ignoring Bramble, and her own fear that Zeke had come to confront them about the break-in.

"You're some kind of magical detectives, right? Saw you following me the other day. I gave you the slip, so you can't be that great. But I kinda need your help."

Fernlight gestured for him to take a seat at her desk. She activated the privacy spell, and then turned to Bramble before joining Zeke. "I don't think he's here to hurt us, but just in case, when you calm down, call Mamoru," she whispered.

Bramble nodded and reached a shaking hand toward the phone.

"When you calm down," she said. "You probably won't make any sense if you call now."

Bramble's hand returned to his side, and he started taking deep breaths. Feeling comfortable that her partner would be all right, Fernlight passed through the privacy spell to join Zeke.

He was slumped in the chair, as if he didn't have the energy to sit straight. His skin had no luster, and while she watched he ran his hands through his hair three times.

"Tell me what the problem is." Fernlight took her own seat. "We'll see if we can help you."

Zeke gnawed at his cuticles for a moment then seemed to realize what he was doing. He dropped his hands to his lap and licked his lips. "Maybe you could tell me why you were following me? You might know something about this already?"

Fernlight wondered if Zeke's need to form everything into a question was part of his state of mind. "We cannot discuss client information."

"I guess that means if you take me on that will apply to me too?"

Fernlight nodded. She waited without speaking, hoping it would prompt Zeke to continue.

"Yeah... Well, it might have to do with your client." He coughed. "Okay, here it is. I created this drug, for this guy, and I probably shouldn't have. I kinda got curious. I don't usually test stuff on myself, because that's how you go crazy in my business. Anyway, like I said I kinda got curious. And I took some of the drug. I thought it was okay, but I gave all of my supply to the buyer. And as soon as it was gone, I started jonesing for it."

Fernlight made some notes on a sheet of paper. "What does jonesing for it mean?"

Zeke became animated, waving his hands at her and bouncing in his seat. "It means I'm addicted. This is what happens, I can't stop this happening ever. I need your help, even if you just send me to someone who can cure me. What I want you to do is destroy the drug. I don't want it on my conscience, whatever he's going to do with it."

Zeke could be very useful in the case. But they had to find something that steadied his nerves, or they couldn't rely on him at all. Fernlight went to the back of the room and searched through their spells to find a tea that would calm him enough, even if it didn't cure his addiction. She watched him as she prepared the water, it took a few moments, but his body stopped moving erratically. When he was still, she saw sweat glistening on his face, and he seemed even thinner than a moment ago.

She handed him the mug. "This might help. Why did you create the drug in the first place?"

Zeke looked at her, surprised. Perhaps he hadn't expected questions. Or perhaps he just realized that she knew about the drug already.

"Why does anyone do anything?" He sipped the tea, making a face at the taste. "Money, and because it was a challenge. I guess there are some things that we shouldn't know."

Fernlight knew that there were Real Folk who had not yet learned that lesson. "Did you create a cure?"

Zeke slammed the mug on the desk. "If I had I wouldn't be here. Stop asking stupid questions. Can you help me, or do I need to go to someone else?"

Fernlight reminded herself that Zeke was addicted to a drug. Perhaps this was his personality, but she decided to give him the benefit of the doubt. "We may be able to help you," she said. "I'm not sure who else you can go to."

Zeke became agitated again. "Let's get started."

She saw Mamoru enter the office. Zeke, sitting with his back to the door, hadn't noticed anything. Fernlight did not want him to become agitated at the sight of someone who was obviously in authority. She added opacity to the privacy spell. "I need to speak with my partner. Please finish your tea, it should help."

"Do you have him restrained?" Mamoru asked, reaching behind his back and bringing handcuffs forward. "I can take him to headquarters, and we will quickly get answers."

"He is taking the drug," Bramble said. "I told you that. How do you know you'll be able to restrain him? He isn't flickering, but who knows if it's about to start. And how are you going to get information from him, when he is half magical?" He stood beside his desk, hands on his hips, waiting for an answer.

Fernlight was tired of the conflict. "He's not restrained. I think he's quite weak, and I'm not sure incarcerating him is the best way to go."

"You are not set up here to deal with such a dangerous person," Mamoru said, but he returned the handcuffs. "Why do you not think we can get the information we need?"

Fernlight didn't know if they were safe for the long term, but she sensed no threat from Zeke. In fact, he radiated weakness and need, rather than danger. "We are at least prepared to use spells. He has reacted well to the calming tea. And I sense no deceit in him. He is frightened, and he wants this to stop. And he wants a cure. Can you provide that to him?"

Mamoru shook his head. "I cannot guarantee that we will be as nurturing as you appear to be. Before I agree to leave him with you, I need to see him."

"Don't upset him. Don't make him mad," Bramble said. "I don't want the Zeke to be angry. Remember Talbot Ryce, and how his flickering increased when he was angry?" Bramble lowered himself to the seat again from where he had flitted up in his sudden fear.

"I only wish to see him," Mamoru said. "No, perhaps that is not true. I wish to ask him questions. We at HOP-D are good at asking questions, do you agree?"

Fernlight could feel control over this case slipping from her hands. She didn't want to deny her client his request, but she feared what would happen if Zeke saw him.

"We will question him together. I think between us we may be able to get the truth, or perhaps even a little information to help us deal with Talbot Ryce." She glanced over her shoulder where she could see Zeke curled over the mug of tea, but she knew Mamoru would just see a wall. "I will tell him what is going to happen. It would not work well if you suddenly appeared in front of him." She didn't wait for an answer, simply slipped through the spell and joined Zeke.

She could see he was getting agitated again, and that he was trying desperately to control it. That worked in his favor.

"What did your partner say? Was he that fairy I saw?"

Zeke's speech patterns were taking on the same shape as Bramble's. If it weren't so dangerous, Fernlight would be fascinated by watching the transition.

"I believe we can both help you, but there is a condition."

"I could pay. I have money."

Fernlight set the kettle to boil again. "We do not need money, but I need you to agree to talk to someone from HOP-D."

"HOP-D? You brought them in. Now they'll kill me. You can't trust them. They want to control everybody." He bounced up from the chair, knocking the mug to the floor in his excitement. The mug was sturdy and didn't shatter on the tiles.

Fernlight kept her movement slow, remaining calm, hoping that Zeke would take some serenity from her. "It is interesting that no one seems to trust HOP-D. I do trust this man. And I will not keep secrets from him."

Fernlight retrieved the mug and added hot water to the herbs left inside. She handed Zeke the tea.

"Do I have a choice?" Zeke took a deep gulp of the tea and winced at the heat as it went down his throat. "Okay, let's get on with it."

Chapter 40

Fernlight added another line to the note she was making. Zeke had given them a fair amount of information, but none of it was organized. She was surprised he'd had the discipline to create a complex spell. Perhaps that was why it wasn't working properly.

An hour ago, Mamoru had convinced Zeke to take protection from HOP-D, and they had left for Zeke's apartment.

"Maybe we should ask Heath about this?" Bramble moved the pieces of paper around on his desk as though trying to make sense of them. "Even without his magic, he knows how to make spells. Fairies don't do this kind of work. Do sprites?"

Fernlight shook her head. "No one does this kind of magic. And we don't have time to run around asking for help from people who are in much the same position as we are. If we had days, or weeks, I would ask the Druids. But you know that they would have to research it."

"Is anyone watching Talbot Ryce? He could be back by now. Even if he was passed out when we left."

Hopelessness draped a heavy cloak around Fernlight's heart. They weren't going to resolve this by reading their notes.

The phone rang, and Bramble picked it up immediately.

"Yes... Yes, we know Heath..." Bramble's eyes widened. "Are you sure?"

Someone spoke on the other side.

"Oh no. Yes, we will come right away."

Bramble took all the notes and put them in a pile. "We have to go to Heath's house. That was the police. He's dead. Hurry."

Fernlight went cold. Heath had become a friend in the last few days. Losing someone was hard for her. If it wasn't for this case, she'd take time to remember him. Bramble's matter of fact attitude made her feel relieved, because she had something to focus on. It also made her angry because he didn't seem to care.

She took a breath. They didn't have time, and it was too much of a coincidence that the only wizard who knew anything about the case was dead. Had Talbot Ryce killed him and absorbed his magic? She'd found it hard to believe that Heath's magic had disappeared altogether. He said it was coming back, so she assumed it was simply inaccessible.

"Did the police say anything else?" She wanted to be prepared when they arrived.

"No. They said we had to come. That they want to ask us questions, and we were the last people he called."

If they already knew who Heath had called, Fernlight was sure that it wasn't simply a natural death. And it took time to trace a call, so it happened at least a couple of hours ago. "Before we go, call Mamoru and let him know what's happened. Since Heath is dead, we don't need to keep him a secret anymore."

While Bramble made the call, Fernlight picked through their supply of charms and spells. With time so short, she wasn't coming back to the office and if they were to confront

Talbot Ryce, they needed spells. One in particular; enough invisibility to last the night.

"I left a message. Are you ready? We should go. I feel very bad for Heath, but I feel even worse for the rest of the world."

WHEN THEY ARRIVED at Heath's, they weren't allowed inside. It seemed as though the investigation was wrapping up because people were carrying things from the house and placing them in vehicles. As they watched, two of the five vehicles pulled away.

A detective came towards them from inside Heath's home. He carried a notebook, and his badge was visible clipped to his belt. "You are Bramble, and Fernlight?"

"I am King Bramble, but yes. Were you expecting another fairy and sprite? We need to get in to see our friend's home. How did he die?"

The detective nodded. "Detective Isaacson. We're almost done inside. I need to ask you some questions. If you find anything that might lead to the killer, you need to tell us."

Fernlight was gratified that he hadn't reacted to Bramble's imperiousness. It seemed like he was all business. "Was he murdered?"

"This is my first case of a wizard dying. If he was human, I would say yes. But let me ask the questions and then you can get inside faster. Okay?"

Fernlight glared at Bramble to stop him from arguing. "What do you need to know?"

"Let's start with the basics. Do you know of anyone who wants your friend dead?"

Fernlight considered. Did she know that Talbot Ryce would want Heath dead? Or would even know who Heath was. "No. Heath was well-respected, but he was working with some humans. I don't know who they were."

"We found some contracts; we'll follow up with them. When did you last see Heath?"

"Yesterday, he wasn't well. And he called us today. But he didn't say anything about being in danger."

Detective Isaacson made a note in his book and closed it. "We have your contact information. We may reach out to you later if we have any more questions. But, off the record, what usually happens if a wizard dies naturally?"

Fernlight had never seen a dead wizard, but she'd heard stories. "They don't usually die of old age. It's often a mistake with an experiment."

"But Heath wasn't doing any experiments. We know his magic wasn't working properly. It must be murder!" Bramble blurted out the words.

Fernlight held her breath. Was detective Isaacson going to follow what he just heard with more questions? It could mean hours of interrogation. Particularly if Isaacson thought they had lied on purpose. When the questions didn't come right away, she relaxed. "There was an earlier slight accident. Heath was recovering. Bramble is right, though, he'd hardly have the power to run an experiment that could kill him."

Detective Isaacson considered them. He looked at his watch and seemed to make a decision. "I need to see you in the morning in my office. Take my card. Nine a.m. sharp."

He turned and walked to a car that was parked outside the ring of official vehicles and drove away.

"I guess that means we go in. I need to see what Heath was doing. Maybe there are some spells left that we can take. Maybe he made some notes." Bramble flitted toward the house.

This is going to get worse, but at least we have a reprieve till tomorrow. If Talbot Ryce wins, interrogation is the least of our worries.

Chapter 41

Fernlight followed Bramble into the room. It was just as messy as before, so there was no way to know if there had been a struggle. "Let's start here," she said, not yet ready to see what had happened in the workroom. "I should have asked where he died."

Bramble was reading the titles of the books on the top shelf of the bookcase. "And we should have asked if they had a wizard here. I bet they didn't think of it. They could have used a spell to recreate everything that happened."

The police had a lot to learn about magical crime. But so did the Real Folk; it wasn't something they did, break the law. Political machinations aside, there were no crimes really. Opening the agency seemed like a way to keep humans from blaming everything on Real Folk — now she wasn't so sure. Was crime contagious?

"We'll suggest it tomorrow," she said. "Let's take advantage of being here first."

"And be quick because we don't have time to help, right? If we tell them now, they might want us to help, and we have to stop Talbot Ryce and save the world." Bramble left the bookshelf and hovered over a box. "This is full of spells," he said. "Maybe we should take them in for safe keeping, and maybe we will need them." He looked up at Fernlight with hope.

She didn't want to remove anything from the scene. "We don't know what will help find the killer. And if they follow our advice, the police will see us on the spell tomorrow."

"Oh. Then why are we here? If we can't take anything that will help us today, then we should go find Talbot Ryce. We do know a little more, and that might make the difference."

And this time they would be invisible, Fernlight thought. "We might find a trace of something. I'm going to test for Heath's magic, there should still be residue, it won't all be absorbed until tonight."

Bramble flitted to join her. "We should do it in his work room. I don't think he did magic out here."

Fernlight nodded. "Are you ready? It might not be pleasant. I think maybe he died there."

"Of course, I am ready. You must learn to be more brave, Fernlight." He zipped ahead of her into the small windowless room.

In the center of the floor was a damp patch of earth. Heath may not have been able to set a circle, or set one properly. If he had, then nothing would have been able to harm him.

"It isn't blood," Bramble said. "Water, maybe, but not blood. And not magic."

Fernlight looked for the salt strings. They were missing, as was the box of salt. "Leave it alone." She went back to the kitchen and brought a shaker of salt. They didn't need to set a circle, but salt was part of the ritual.

"Bramble, come and help me." She felt tears pushing the backs of her eyes. Heath's dream of a future with convenient magic was gone. No one else seemed to be willing to change from the old ways. No Real Folk at least. A human might be interested but would have no power to fuel it.

Bramble brought a few sprigs of rosemary and handful of ground beetles. "I can do the words if you are crying too much. You just mix and light the powder when it's time."

Fernlight happily let Bramble lead the spell. Fairies had such short lives that they were more comfortable with death than most Real Folk. Sprites rarely lost a friend. They lived for many years, growing larger with each season. When they came to the end, they simply crumbled back into the soil.

At the right point in the chant, Fernlight lit the small pile of powder. The flame flashed high, turning amber and then clear and then blue. The result should have been wisps of wizard magic floating near the ground. All Fernlight saw was a trace of smoke as the powder was consumed.

"He didn't have magic! Maybe it wasn't Heath! We should have asked the detective if we could see the body!" Bramble was floating up and down in his excitement.

Fernlight refused to let herself hope. She took out her phone and called the detective. "Are you sure it is Heath?"

"It was a wizard, and he matched Heath's description." He paused. Fernlight could hear people talking in the background. "Let me call you back in a minute."

"Well?" Bramble asked. "Is he sure? Should we keep looking for something to help, or should we try to find Heath?"

Fernlight told him what the detective reported. "There's something else, but we have to wait. Let's keep looking." The hope she suppressed grew too strong to ignore. If they were certain, then the Detective would not have said he'd call back.

The workroom was clear. Whoever had committed the murder was smart enough to take all of the regular spell craft tools. She joined Bramble in the living room and surveyed the mess. "We can look for a half hour, but we need to move on after that."

Her phone rang and she hit the accept picture.

"We could use confirmation. Can I send you a picture of the body?"

Fernlight put the phone on speaker. "How badly damaged is it?" She had no desire to look at a body so badly mutilated it was unidentifiable.

"Not a mark on him. Whoever did this knew how to kill without making a mess." The words were flat as though the detective didn't know what emotion to feel.

"Okay." She went to press end call, but Bramble stopped her.

"Are you going to send it by text?" He shouted into the speaker.

"Yeah, you don't need to yell."

"You don't need to stop talking. You can press here, and then here. When he sends the picture, you can look at it and keep talking."

The phone beeped as Bramble stopped speaking. "Look, there it is. Tap it and we'll see it bigger."

Fernlight didn't need to see a larger picture. "It's Heath." Tears started flowing again. The pain of loss stronger because of the moments of hope.

"Thanks. I'll see you tomorrow in my office." The call ended.

Chapter 42

"That was very rude. He didn't even say goodbye. I'm sorry that it was Heath. I can do the searching if you want to sit and be sad for a while." Bramble wanted to give Fernlight a hug, but she was far too big for his arms.

Fernlight wiped her eyes and then shook her head. "I'll take some time after the case. It'll be faster if we both search."

Now that she was back to being his normal Fernlight, Bramble could turn away and concentrate on the search. He had no idea what they would find, but there might be all kinds of things that should be kept away from the humans as they investigate. "I will take care of this side of the room," he said, pointing to the back near the workroom. "And you do the rest. That way you don't have to see where he died again and maybe you won't be so sad."

Fernlight gave him a smile. It wasn't her usual big smile but it made him feel better.

There were a lot of shelves of books for him to look through. There were things on the floor, and some of the shelves were two books deep. He would not be able to search all of them in the little time they had. But he could look at the books that Heath had been using recently. Those were the ones with less dust on them.

Starting in the top far left corner, Bramble made his way right. At the end of the shelf, he floated down one level and moved left. His plan was to take out any interesting books and place them on the floor until he had searched every shelf.

On the first pass, he found three books that had been pulled out recently. He didn't stop to look at them, just placed them in a separate pile on the floor. By the time he reached the lowest shelf he had ten books.

"There doesn't seem to be anything of interest here," Fernlight said.

Bramble did not want her helping him, because she might mix up the books, and he had a system. "What about the kitchen? Why don't you check in there and the bathroom while I look through this? I will not be long, I promise."

He heard her move into the other room but didn't look up. Digging through the books on the floor didn't add anything to his pile of items to check. So he started flipping through each of the ten books; three were histories of ancient wizards, two were simply lists of spells and where they could be found, and the rest were old notebooks of Heath's. Bramble slipped those five into his bag. If the police saw him tomorrow in the spell — if they cast the spell to watch the action — it would be okay to give them back. *If we're alive, anyway.* Then he joined Fernlight in the kitchen. She was holding three syringes in her hand. And reading something in the book spread on the counter.

Bramble flew to look over her shoulder. "Is it a cure? Are those needles how we cure the people who have taken this drug? Have we solved the case?"

Fernlight slipped the syringes into her own bag. She held the book open to a page and pointed. "The missing ingredient is blood," she read. "'Combining the contents of the syringes with blood from a human who is addicted to the original drug will cure the addiction.'"

Bramble read the lines again. "You forgot to read this part. It says 'untested'."

Fernlight closed the book and slipped it into her bag along with the syringes already nestled inside. "He seems pretty certain. He doesn't say it *may* he says it *will* cure, and I guess we're the ones who are going to test it." Fernlight headed for the door.

"Do you think that's why Heath is dead? That he tested this cure on himself. Because he took the drug earlier. And that's why it's a human addict?"

"We won't know until we test it. At least now when we find Talbot Ryce, we have something to do." Fernlight locked the door. "We can also ask Zeke what he thinks."

FERNLIGHT DIDN'T CARE what the humans thought, this was too important to worry about appearances. She and Bramble moved at the speed of Real Folk until they stood outside Zeke's home. The door was still locked, so she buzzed his apartment since he might be expecting them anyway. There was no answer.

"I thought that there would be a policeman here. In the lobby, I mean. But I guess they meant outside his door, or maybe inside with him." Bramble was flitting back and forth in front of the window, peering into the back of the lobby.

"Unlock the door, Bramble. We don't have time to wait for someone to answer the buzzer." Fernlight wondered if pressing the buzzer would have any effect if Zeke and the policeman guarding him were in the lab. Perhaps Zeke himself was looking for a cure.

Bramble placed his hand against the door and Fernlight

heard a click. They raced through the lobby, ignoring the elevator and running for the stairs.

"Can I unlock the door to his apartment too, or are we going to have to sneak in?"

Mamoru would have something to say about them breaking in, but Fernlight needed to talk to Zeke now. She would explain it to the policeman inside. But knocking on the door if they were in the lab would likely not bring their attention.

Fernlight gestured to the lock as they approached the door. "Just go ahead and unlock it. Don't break it though."

Bramble held his hand out to cast a spell, but he dropped it and turned to look up at Fernlight. "It's already unlocked, I think there might be something wrong. Maybe Talbot Ryce has been here first. Maybe he's inside, and we can stop him now."

Fernlight reached over Bramble's head and turned the door handle. Stepping inside she saw that the apartment looked very like it had the last time. It felt empty of any presence. "They must be in the lab." She started walking towards the hidden door, when she felt Bramble tugging at her sleeve.

"If Talbot Ryce is there, it could be a trap. Should we both go, or should I stay here in case you need me to rescue you?"

"If we go in quietly, we will surprise him. It would be better for both of us to be there, I think. That way no one will need rescuing." She hoped the last words were true.

Bramble flitted ahead of her, sliding into the staircase and waiting inside. As Fernlight slipped through, the thought that it could be a trap resurfaced. Her confidence wavered, but having no other plan, she simply followed Bramble up the stairs.

It was clear there was no one there as soon as she stepped into the room. While it was large it was also open, and the sun shone through the windows. Fernlight was sure that Mamoru meant Zeke to stay in his home. But perhaps she had misunderstood.

Chapter 43

She pulled out her phone and dialed Mamoru's number, hitting speaker so that Bramble would be able to hear the whole conversation.

Mamoru answered after half a ring. "What do you need?"

He had been terse before, but now she felt the time pressure they were all experiencing. "We're at Zeke's home."

"You found something?" Mamoru's question came before Fernlight could provide any more information.

"No, in fact no one is here." Fernlight realized that she was touching her bag where the potential cure resided.

"He is supposed to be there," Mamoru said. "Is Constable Riverton there? What does he have to say?"

Fernlight picked up the phone from the table where she had placed it, and beckoned Bramble to follow her. There was no point in spending more time here and Mamoru would have to find Zeke. "I meant no one at all. Your constable is missing; we'll leave that to you. We have to find Talbot Ryce." She ended the call before Mamoru could say anything.

When they reached Zeke's front door, Fernlight asked

Bramble to make sure it was locked behind them. There was no need to make the apartment easy to get into.

As they ran down the stairs, Fernlight's phone rang again. It was Mamoru.

"I don't have anything to help you find Zeke. At least right now; once we're done with Talbot, we can help you." She reached to end the call as they slipped through the stairs into the lobby.

"Wait," Mamoru's voice came through loudly. She had never heard him yell before.

"I'm still here." On the street, she pointed Bramble toward the nearest magical path.

"Talbot Ryce is in his home. We are observing him at the moment. Would you like our men to join you inside?"

"They will only be in danger; we'll go inside by ourselves." Bramble was flying just in front of Fernlight so that he could speak into the phone. "We will be traveling in a way that does not allow us to take phone calls." He looked at Fernlight grinning. "We will call you back when we have some information." He stabbed his finger at the screen, ending the call. "That should give us some privacy for long enough to try to cure Talbot Ryce."

They entered the park and said the words that would open the magical path.

A FEW MINUTES LATER, they exited the magical path close to Talbot Ryce's house again. Fernlight looked around, it would be good to know where Mamoru's men were just in case they needed help. Halfway down the street, parked under an ancient Chestnut tree, two men sat in a car. "Do they think that they are invisible? Surely anyone in the neighborhood would notice that they were surveilling someone. There isn't anybody else parked on the street."

Bramble glanced over to where she pointed. "Should we go talk to them? If we need help, they should know when to come in. Think about how easy it would be to surveil someone, if they could become invisible. That's probably another thing Heath could've done. Maybe we should give ideas to wizards as a sideline."

Fernlight wasn't in the mood to discuss any new businesses. This one case may kill them. "Let's just worry about getting ourselves inside the house. I took ten invisibility spells."

"That should be enough, at least for today. Let's get started."

Fernlight passed a spell package to Bramble. There was no point in being invisible when they got into the house if he saw them come from the street.

Bramble released his spell at the same time she did. The familiar feeling that it wasn't working came over her. "Go towards the car and see if they notice you."

Bramble looked at her, questions on his face. "As soon as this case is over, I am going to talk to a wizard about building in something to the spell that will tell us we are invisible. I remember a time, was it only a few days ago? We never questioned whether the spell was working or not." He flew toward the car and then circled it waving wildly through the windshield. The men didn't react.

Feeling slightly more confident, Fernlight led the way around back of the house. Going into the kitchen again would at least put them on familiar territory. And she couldn't imagine someone like Talbot Ryce even making himself a cup of tea, so they would be safe for a few seconds.

This time Fernlight could feel a presence in the house; downstairs, where they had found the picture.

"It feels like two people," Bramble said. "I wasn't expecting that. Maybe we should ask the humans outside to come and help. I might not be able to take on a whole human by myself.

Especially if it's Talbot Ryce." He crept toward the door to the downstairs room.

Fernlight wasn't ready yet to ask for help. "We should just go look," she whispered. "It would be better to ask for help when we know what we need help with."

Bramble was trembling already, but he seemed unwilling to admit his fear. "Do you remember if this door creaked? There's no point in being invisible if he can hear us, he'll know something is happening."

Someone shouted from downstairs, and another one cried out in pain.

"He probably won't notice. But if I go through it, the door will have to open quite wide. Do you think that you could go down and look and come back?"

Bramble's eyes widened and his trembling increased. "How will you know to come help me? If you are up here and I am down there and something goes wrong, you might be too late."

Fernlight wasn't surprised that Bramble was so reluctant. She would not have been eager to go down by herself. "Okay, we go together. Let me open the door slowly, and if the shouting happens again, I'll open it fast. Then no one will hear us."

There was no convenient shouting, but the door opened quietly enough to let her slip through. She stepped down, feeling Bramble pressed up behind her, and saw Talbot Ryce with his back to her standing over Zeke. What they had heard were the results of torture. Zeke's body was bathed in sweat, and there was blood sliding down his bare arms.

She stepped backward up the stair, and Bramble hurried to the door. By the time she got there it was open, and he was through.

Talbot Ryce might be focused on the damage he was doing to Zeke, but Fernlight wanted to be as far away from the door to the basement as she could be. If he overheard them talking, it would draw his attention to them. And what she had to say couldn't be done in whispers.

She led Bramble to the upstairs rooms. The one with the exercise equipment had a padded floor that was likely to muffle their words.

"We have to rescue Zeke. He's too important," she said quietly.

Bramble flew to the window which looked down onto the street. "I think it's time to bring those humans in. It's not safe for us to try and rescue Zeke."

Fernlight had to agree about the safety, but Talbot Ryce was too far along in his transition for humans to take him into custody. "I think they will just get in the way," she said. "It's going to be hard enough to rescue Zeke, I don't want us in a position where we have to rescue two other humans as well."

"I wish we could just leave. Maybe this is better left to the Druids. They are much braver." Bramble seemed to be making an attempt to get his trembling under control, but to Fernlight it looked like an epic battle.

"I could call them through the trees, but they don't understand what's going on. We would have to explain everything. And by that time Talbot Ryce will be done with Zeke." A plan was forming in her mind as she spoke. Rescuing Zeke could wait. Once they overcame Talbot Ryce, he would be safe.

"I am afraid, but I will try to be brave. I have to think about my people, I must remember that it is my responsibility as king to protect them." Fernlight saw him gain control as he spoke; the frantic pace of his wings slowing, his voice dropping into a more comfortable range for her ears. "Should we just overcome him? If we ran at him, like we did in the cabin, I could scratch at his face and you could knock him over. Then we could tie him up."

Her partner now feeling more confident, Fernlight was ready to act. "I'm not sure we can count on that same thing happening again. We need to go down there, go into the room and see what's happening. If we can, knocking Talbot Ryce over will at least stop him from torturing Zeke. But once we touch him, he will know we are there and being invisible might not be an advantage."

Chapter 44

By the time they made it to the basement room, Zeke had screamed three more times. Each time a little shriller and a little weaker. Now they stood looking at the two men. Talbot Ryce standing over Zeke with a club; Zeke bruised and bleeding. Bramble no longer jammed against Fernlight's back, stood beside her as if he was afraid to let his wings start up the panic again. They couldn't speak because there was no way they wouldn't be overheard, and disembodied voices would be as much of a problem as actually being seen. As would taking any weapons to help them knock Talbot Ryce out.

She reached over and tapped Bramble's shoulder and held up three fingers. She curled each finger into her palm slowly. And then they both rushed Talbot Ryce.

"How did you get in here?"

Fernlight stumbled to a stop.

Talbot Ryce was looking directly at them.

"Tell that fairy to get back here," he said, pointing over her shoulder.

Fernlight turned around to see Bramble disappearing through the door.

"You can see us," she said. "We are supposed to be invisible."

Zeke lifted his head and looked around the room. "Who the fuck is talking?" His voice was strained and his head dropped as he said the words.

At least the spell hadn't failed, it must have something to do with how far along in the transition Talbot Ryce was.

"You'd better let him go," Fernlight said, pointing at Zeke. "My partner's gone to get help. It won't be long before this place is overrun with police." There was a little tremor in her voice that seemed to betray her confident words.

"Do you really think I care? You send all the cops you want. Half of them are in my pocket anyway. As to the rest? Well, I'm pretty sure that I can deal with anyone with magic. I'm really surprised that you folk have not taken over." As he spoke, he moved towards Fernlight, whose feet were rooted in the spot. He'd used more of the drug, or had found a way to test his theory, because while he still flickered, he stayed human less and less.

"Is that why you murdered Heath?" she asked, trying to get her legs to work.

"Who is that?" Ryce asked.

"A wizard." She struggled and felt her left foot move a little. "A friend."

"I didn't kill him. I wish I had, then the transformation would be complete." He glanced at Zeke. "This one is probably useless, but I'm enjoying the process."

Fernlight tried to move, even if it was simply to a different place in the room. Anything to delay him until Bramble brought help. She took a few steps to the side, but it was an effort.

"Oh, don't bother trying to run," Talbot Ryce said, reaching for her arm. "I may not be able to cast a spell yet, but you must remember I have bought a few."

Fernlight set her feet and resisted his tug. He may be able to slow her down, but she still outweighed him, and any sprite was stronger than a human, if it came to a fight.

He grunted with the effort to drag her towards Zeke. He let her arm go and shrugged. "Fine. Stay there, I can bring what I need to you."

Fernlight went cold, as though her blood had drained into the floor. She watched as he went to the desk and picked up a syringe.

"I was going to try and use this on Zeke, because I understand he's been dipping into my drug. I just don't think my theory will hold up using someone whose blood isn't pure magic."

"I thought your theory was that you would kill Real Folk to absorb their magic," Fernlight said. If she could anger him, perhaps he would make a mistake. Or at least she could delay the inevitable.

"Yes, but death is so permanent. Let's first try a little blood transfusion."

Zeke struggled in the chair, trying to release himself from the bonds. "Is that Fernlight? You have to run. He's been trying to get me to tell him how to make the conversion. I can't get him to believe that I don't know."

Fernlight wondered if Zeke would be an ally. If she could free herself from the spell, would she be able to release him. And even if she did, would he have the strength to fight alongside her, or would he just get in the way?

Talbot Ryce returned to her side and reached for her arm. She flailed and managed to punch his shoulder, but he held on to the syringe.

"Keep fighting, I am sure you'll tire before I do."

Fernlight punched out again, this time Talbot dodged. And then he grabbed her arm, twisting it so that her elbow was pointing to the floor. He peered at the skin while dodging her other arm as she tried to tear him away.

"Don't you have any veins?" He twisted her arm around as far as he could. "How do I get your blood? Why is this so freaking hard?"

Fernlight wrenched her arm out of his grasp and tried to take his other arm to flip him onto the ground. Talbot Ryce was too fast for her. He seemed to understand what she was going to do before she even thought of it. That was not magic.

"Stay there." Talbot Ryce went to his computer, opened it up, and started typing. "I'm sure there must be something on sprite anatomy on the Internet by now."

Trying to keep both men in her sight, Fernlight dug in her bag for a counter spell. Talbot Ryce looked at her, laughed, and then went back to his search.

Zeke had managed to free his arm, and now he was stretching to undo the knots that held his other arm and his legs. Talbot Ryce seem to have lost interest in Zeke.

"Ah, I see." Talbot Ryce moved to her side again, knocking the little packets from her hand. "You won't find a counter spell in time. Now, it says that the best way to draw blood from a sprite is to press on the chin, and a vein will appear along the jawline."

His arm came forward and Fernlight leaned back as far she could. "How do you know that information is correct? I understand the Internet is full of lies."

Where is Bramble?

"Very true, but we will see in a moment." He ducked under her arm and grabbed her chin.

Chapter 45

Bramble watched from his position near the stairs. He knew he should go and get help, but humans wouldn't be any help. Fernlight had been right about that. It was up to him. If he could cure Talbot Ryce, then he could fly and get the humans, because then they would be able to help.

His wings started twitching in terror again. *STOP IT!* He didn't have time to be scared. Everything was going to be very complicated. They should have split up the syringes that they took from Heath's house. He had to get Talbot Ryce's blood. And then he had to get the syringes, or maybe it should be the other way around, and mix the potion, and stab Talbot Ryce.

He scanned the room again, hoping for some ideas of how to get started. Would it be helpful if Zeke could see him? Or would Zeke let Talbot Ryce know that Bramble was sneaking up on him.

Fairies didn't need to be invisible to be good at sneaking. But he would probably only have one chance.

Talbot Ryce was fighting with Fernlight, trying to get her blood. Zeke was getting free.

Bramble couldn't think anymore. He reversed the invisibility spell and buzzed into the room. He circled Zeke and placed a knife from the desk into his hand. Talbot Ryce was so busy trying to kill Fernlight, that he didn't know Bramble was there.

Bramble could see the scratches on Talbot Ryce's face from their earlier fight. He needed more than just scratches this time. And he also needed something to catch the blood so he could put it in the syringe. He didn't have a lot of time to think, Talbot Ryce would know he was there any second.

He looked on the desk and saw a flat thing like a saucer that had indents around the side. That would do perfectly. He buzzed away as Talbot Ryce swiped at him with his free hand.

The Zeke was free!

Bramble picked up the saucer and shouted, "Help me. Cut him."

Zeke rushed towards Talbot Ryce, who was still entangled with Fernlight. Bramble could see the vein pulsing on Fernlight's jaw; Talbot Ryce would have her blood any second.

Zeke ducked under the flailing arms and stuck the knife into Talbot Ryce's thigh. Before he pulled it out, he twisted it. Talbot Ryce screamed, and lost his grip on Fernlight as his leg buckled. Before he could fall to the ground Bramble rushed in and gathered a few spoonfuls of the blood dripping from the wound.

"Give me a syringe. Quick, before he stands up again," he shouted as Talbot Ryce put weight on the leg again and started to rise.

Fernlight was gasping for breath, but she slid her hand into the bag and tossed one syringe to Bramble. And then slipped her bag over her shoulder and tossed it into the corner.

While Bramble's attention was away from him, Talbot Ryce had regained his footing. Bramble watched in horror as the man lunged and toppled his partner. Fernlight's eyes closed as her head hit the ground.

"Bramble, hurry," the Zeke shouted.

His trance was broken, and he saw that Talbot Ryce was more interested in tying Fernlight up than coming after him. Knowing it wouldn't last, he dipped the tip of the syringe into the little pool of blood and pulled back the plunger. Or tried to pull back the plunger. It wouldn't work.

"Give it to me," the Zeke said and grabbed both items from Bramble.

The Zeke pulled off the pointy end, and Bramble could see underneath was a metal needle.

"How much blood do I need?"

Bramble shrugged. "The notes didn't say, but don't use all of it. We might need a second dose." He didn't want to tell Zeke that it might be a cure because if it didn't work then Zeke would be upset. And also, Talbot Ryce did not need to know what was in the needle.

Bramble heard a grunt behind him. And saw Talbot Ryce rising again, clearly satisfied that Fernlight would not be able to escape.

Bramble looked at the syringe. The Zeke had finished, and now the fluid was purple. "Give it to me." The Zeke obeyed without question, and then moved away looking frightened.

"Give me that," Talbot Ryce said as he reached to snatch the syringe from Bramble's hand.

Bramble's wings started trembling again, but he told them to stop. They didn't stop like they did before, but they got a little more calm. Bramble flitted away from Talbot Ryce's reach.

"No. And be careful. This is poison. Undo my friend, or I will stab you with this." He made the motion with the needle like it was a dart.

Talbot Ryce hesitated, perhaps he believed Bramble. Blood was still flowing from his leg, so he must be getting weak. But what was more frightening was the fact that he now stayed in the magic phase almost all the time.

Bramble tried to keep track of everyone. Zeke was out of his line of sight, and he couldn't risk turning away to check on him. He hoped the human had the sense to stay out of the way.

It didn't seem to matter to Talbot Ryce what Bramble did, anyway. He turned around to look at Fernlight, who was still tied and seemed to be unconscious. Talbot moved a step towards Fernlight, then turned to Bramble.

"You two are very lucky," he said, his words crackling with power. "You are about to witness the moment the world changes. It is a pity you will not be able to tell anyone, because as soon as I have power, I will kill you. I can't have witnesses interfering with my plans. At least not until after tonight."

Bramble didn't know if it was simply his fear, or a spell, but no matter what he said, his wings trembled, and his heart fluttered as long as Talbot Ryce stared at him. But as soon as the man turned away, Bramble gained control again.

"Stay away from her. Don't hurt her. I will really stick this in you. Maybe this is what we witness, your death." Before either of the humans could do anything to stop him, Bramble rushed forward until he was hovering at Talbot Ryce's back. He tried to stick the needle in his arm, but Talbot Ryce just waved him away. It was like the man knew without looking exactly where Bramble was. Maybe he already had magic, and it was too late to cure him.

He dodged and continued interrupting Talbot Ryce as he tried to bring Fernlight's vein to the surface again, Bramble tried to see a place to stick the needle in but Talbot Ryce's movements were too fast even for a fairy.

"Help me, Zeke" Bramble yelled.

Bramble flew towards Fernlight. Perhaps he would find a

way to get between Talbot Ryce's hands and do both things; save Fernlight and poke Talbot Ryce.

"You are in my way, fairy. Leave me alone and I promise I won't hurt you." Talbot Ryce stopped reaching for Fernlight and tried to catch Bramble in his hands.

"Why don't you try fighting me?" Zeke stepped towards Talbot Ryce. He managed to grab and hold onto one of the man's arms. "I'm not as fragile as a fairy. Maybe when you're magic, it'll be fair. Right now, you look like a fucking asshole."

Bramble heard Fernlight groan, but he couldn't stop. This was his chance! He flew toward Talbot Ryce, whose arm was exposed as he struggled with the Zeke. He raised the needle ready to stab. Zeke stopped pulling and pushed suddenly. Talbot Ryce moved and Bramble hit his neck. He didn't think, he just pressed the plunger. When Bramble pulled away, he saw Zeke move in and use the knife he'd given him to slice deeper into Talbot Ryce's neck.

Blood flew everywhere.

Chapter 46

Fernlight watched Talbot Ryce fall. He flickered once into the magic, and then the blue light slid from his body as soon as he touched the ground. Like a slick of oil that was alive, it soaked into the carpet and then drained through.

The room was silent.

"Can you untie me? This is really uncomfortable." She tried to wiggle into a sitting position, but the ropes cut at her skin.

Zeke snapped to life at her words. "I can't actually see you," he said.

She reversed the invisibility spell. He ran over and sliced through the ropes, then held out his hand to pull her to her feet. Fernlight was grateful; even such a short time in that position had stiffened her body.

She walked to where Bramble still stood looking at the body, the syringe still somehow in his hand, still half full. She touched his shoulder and took the weapon away from him.

He blinked and looked at her. "Did we cure him? Was that the drug sliding into the earth? Did we poison the earth?" He flew to where Zeke was rolling Talbot Ryce's body over. "You shouldn't have killed him. Now we don't know if the cure works. And maybe we made it worse."

Zeke looked from Bramble to Fernlight and back again. There was no remorse in his expression, no anger, but his eyes flickered from brown to glowing blue. Around him the stain that had soaked into the carpet started to rise again, seeping around the body like a moat.

"Zeke, stand up and walk away from him, please," Fernlight said, trying to keep the panic from her voice.

Then Bramble noticed what she'd seen. "Yes! Zeke, run, get away from the body. We have to catch the magic. We don't know what it'll do if it goes back into the ground, too many Real Folk get their power from there."

"What are you talking about?" Zeke asked as he stepped away from the body. "How are you going to capture magic, and what magic do you mean?"

Fernlight waited until he was outside of the growing stain. "You can't see that?" She pointed to the carpet.

"Yeah, but dead bodies release their contents; that's urine not magic, right?" He moved further away from it. "It's going to start stinking in here soon. We should go. And I don't know about you, but I don't want to be caught here and have to answer questions."

As Zeke moved closer to the stairs, the stain shifted toward him, no longer a circle of darker color in the carpet, it started to look like a teardrop with the end pointing at Zeke.

"That's not normal. It's following me. You have to do something." Zeke looked around. "Fucking everything is carpeted." He climbed on top of the desk. "Do something."

Fernlight looked at the syringe in her hand. If it was a cure, would it be better to test it on the carpet to see if it stopped the movement?

"I said you shouldn't have killed him." Bramble hovered above the liquid in the carpet. "It's the magic, I can feel it, and it's bad. There's something wrong, magic should go back into the universe. This is seeking a victim." He flew to the Zeke and joined him on the table. "If we knew it was a cure, we would give it to you and maybe the magic would stop finding you and go look for one of your other drug takers. But right now, we don't know."

Fernlight backed away as the magic moved in her direction. There was no room for her on the desk with the other two. If she ran, she could leave Zeke there. Bramble would follow her. They could ask the local real folk if anything had happened while the magic was in the soil. But by the time they got back, it could be too late for Zeke. And only he knew who else was taking the drug.

"We don't know how much of this it will take to cure you. This might not be enough, but if you know other people who are addicted, we can create more." She looked at the stain again, but apparently it had decided that Real Folk were not the target. At least there was some good in the situation. "Bramble, go outside and find out from the Privet Fairies if there was any effect when it seeped into the ground."

It took only a minute for Bramble to come back. "They were very scared, but they watched it. They said it didn't disappear, but it started moving. It was very slow, and it moved back and forth, like it was looking for something. And then suddenly it went back to where it came from. I told the men in the car to call Mamoru."

The something it was looking for was probably another addict, Fernlight decided. If she was right, then they needed to test the cure on Zeke. But they also needed some of his blood, because if this was a cure they needed to make more. "Good, we will need him soon. Did you use all of his blood?" she asked Bramble.

"No, but what's left is all sludgy. I don't think it will work to make another dose."

"How many people took the drug?" As she asked, she noticed that the stain had reached the desk, and was crawling up the leg. Apparently, that material wasn't as helpful as the carpet. The stain couldn't make purchase. But there was no way now for Zeke to leave without touching it.

Zeke was staring in horror at the floor; the flickering that had only been in his eyes before was now twitching throughout his body. He looked up at Fernlight, and she saw tears falling.

"Three. I only gave it to three other people." He looked wildly between Fernlight and Bramble. "I don't know how they knew about it, but the money was good."

"Bramble, take the saucer and the knife upstairs and clean them and then come back," Fernlight said.

The flickering throughout Zeke's body increased. They'd seen this happen with Talbot Ryce when he became agitated or angry, but she couldn't help feeling as though the damp stain beneath the desk was causing it.

Zeke looked at his hands, and then touched them to his face. "I can feel it. It doesn't hurt, and I'm pretty sure it won't hurt if I step into that pool." He lowered himself to sit on the top of the desk and clutched the sides. "I don't know how long I can wait; you need to do something now."

Fernlight wished she could reach Zeke. The strain of not stepping down and answering the call of power must be agony. Sweat slipped from under his hair, down his face and onto the desk.

"Okay, it's here." Bramble announced as he landed on the desk beside Zeke. "You look worse. This is going fast. If you are cured, it will go seeking the others. Are there any close?"

"One downtown. The other two were on the North Shore. How quickly can you get there?"

"Not fast enough, but this stain may have difficulty crossing the water. But I have an idea, and we have an extra syringe.

Bramble, cut him and collect the blood. More than you did from Talbot Ryce."

Zeke held out his arm and pointed to a blue vein. "It will be faster from here," he said, his voice shaky. "But you might have to seal it afterward, because I could bleed out." As he spoke his eyes kept going back to the carpet.

"Okay Bramble, we have a healing spell in my bag. Get that, and two syringes, and then cut him." Fernlight didn't want to say what her idea was, it felt cruel to give Zeke false hope. And she didn't even know if it was a cure.

She watched as Bramble gathered the blood, pressed the healing stone on Zeke's arm, and created a mixture in the two syringes.

"If this works, we need his blood," Bramble said as he placed the cap on the extra syringe. "It will probably go gloopy like the other sample. Should I just mix all of the syringes?"

"We'll work fast. I'm sure the blood will be good until we know if it's a cure."

Bramble held up the syringe. "Should I give him all of it?"

"Let me do it," Zeke said, his hand reaching for the syringe. "If it's a cure, I think I'll feel it. I'll give myself a little bit and leave the syringe in. And if it doesn't cure me right away, I'll give myself a little bit more. Until the syringes are empty. I assume that once that's done, we'll know if it's a cure, or if I'm still fucked."

Fernlight nodded for Bramble to hand the syringe to Zeke. "Before you do, we need to know who else took the drug."

Bramble took a piece of paper out of his pocket along with a pencil. Zeke gave him the names, and phone numbers.

"Okay, here I go." Zeke inserted the needle into another thick blue vein. He pushed the plunger, putting about a quarter of the contents into his body.

The room was silent, so much so that Fernlight assumed everyone was holding their breath like she was.

Zeke shook his head, and then pressed until half of the liquid was in his body. He closed his eyes, and all the tension left his body. And then, before anyone could react, he fell from the desktop to the floor.

Bramble was hovering above him before anything else happened. "He still breathing. He's not dead, that's good, and look! The stain is moving away. It's a cure." He started pinching Zeke and shouting, "wake up, wake up."

This time the stain was moving faster. Fernlight rushed to Zeke's body, pulled out the needle, and sprayed the rest of the contents over the stain before it returned to the dead body on the floor.

It stopped moving. Everywhere a droplet of blood hit the magic in the carpet, steam rose. She could see the magic separating from the water in the steam and returning to the earth clean and pure.

Shaking with relief, she took the other syringe and emptied it onto the remaining stain. Rubbing it in to encompass the rest of the evil magic.

THEY SAT with Zeke and waited until Mamoru arrived.

It wasn't long before they heard the back door slam closed, and moments later Mamoru strode down the stairs. When he got to the bottom, he didn't say anything at first. He looked around, noted Talbot Ryce's body, and then came to the corner where Fernlight, Bramble, and Zeke waited.

"Tell me what happened, and do it quickly. I need to know what the police will see, and I need to know how to protect you." He pulled on some blue latex gloves as he spoke.

Fernlight stood and waited until the other two joined her. It was hard to know how well to streamline the information when she didn't know what the police might want. Perhaps that was another area of their preparation that she had neglected.

"Ryce tried to kill us," Zeke said. "It was an accident. His death, I mean. We were trying to cure him. And he fought us. The cure works; they used it on me, and I am totally back to normal."

Fernlight glanced at Bramble to see if he was going to contradict the story. He had on his innocent face.

Mamoru looked Zeke over and finally nodded. "Normal for a drug dealer. Would anyone have seen you?"

"The men in the car." Fernlight didn't think Mamoru meant Real Folk with his question. "Bramble talked to them, so even if they hadn't seen us come in because of the invisibility spell, they knew we were here. And I guess they knew something was wrong."

Mamoru strode over to Talbot Ryce's body and turned him over. "Those men are with me. They won't tell the police anything."

With Talbot Ryce's body facing up, Fernlight could see the gash in his neck, and the blood drying across his chest. She couldn't leave Mamoru thinking that it was solved. Zeke had promised to deal with the other addicts, but the longer he was away from his cure, the more the money might make the difference, and he'd start making more of the drug. "There are others and we have the cure."

"Yeah. I'm going to make sure they get cured," Zeke said.

Mamoru turned Talbot Ryce face down again, and made an adjustment so it didn't look like he'd been moved at all. "And how much will you charge them?"

Fernlight saw Zeke grin. "They're very rich men. And there's no more drug, so they'll be hurting. It's not a crime for me to make a little profit."

Mamoru removed the gloves and stuck them in his pocket. "It *is* a crime. Both the drug and the cure are illegal. When we leave, you will go with the two men in the car. And they will assist you in curing your clients."

"What will happen now?" Bramble asked. "There's a dead body, and you are going to leave it here, right? What if there's something here that ties us to the crime?" Bramble was flitting back and forth across the room in his agitation. "Maybe we should get rid of the body."

Mamoru directed them up the stairs into the kitchen. "This is what will happen. The police will be called later today with an anonymous tip. Before that happens, someone will come and make sure there's no evidence that you were here. Fern-light and Bramble, you will go back to your office and wait for me to call you. Zeke, you will cure your clients. And you will get out of the drug business." He stared at Zeke until the man nodded.

"Any questions you have must wait until later." He drew his phone from his pocket, held the kitchen door open for them, and nodded for them to go through.

Chapter 47

It took a couple of days for Mamoru to contact them. Fernlight had closed the office for a whole day. Bramble had gone home, to restore his energy, conduct his business as king, and probably tell his wife everything. Fernlight had gone to the forest and met with Beacon. To her surprise he agreed that while she had cases, she would be exempt from working with the plants. And she was welcome to restore herself without worry.

The second day they spent in the office, Bramble's son, Briar, buzzing around asking questions about everything and anything he saw.

Mamoru walked in midmorning on the third day since they had left Talbot Ryce's house. Both of Bramble's children were in the office, and both hid under his desk at the sight of the human.

"Do not be afraid, children," Bramble said bending down to talk to them. "This is the human I told you about. He will not hurt you." A couple of undecipherable squeaks came as a response. "Then stay there, I'm sure you will get used to him very quickly. After all, I did."

Mamoru chose the client chair at her desk, Fernlight

noticed. Now that she knew him better, she was sure it was in deference to the children's fear.

"Did you read the news this morning?" Mamoru asked.

Fernlight and Bramble had been reading the headlines on the Internet. Talbot Ryce's body had been found. There were no suspects, but the police were investigating it as a homicide.

"Yes," Fernlight said.

Mamoru reached into his jacket pocket and took out an envelope. "Here is the fee we agreed on. And I wish to speak to you about the future."

"Do you have a new case for us? Now that we are rested, we want to investigate what happened to Heath. It's not right that his death should go uninvestigated. And humans probably can't figure it out. It's going to take a Real Folk. And we are the ones who know how to investigate," Bramble said.

Mamoru smoothed his jacket, a move Fernlight knew meant he was nervous. Was he going to discourage them from looking into Heath's death? Was it something that his organization wanted kept secret? The way they had kept secret what happened to Talbot Ryce.

"At HOP-D, we are fully aware of our reputation. Talbot Ryce's actions did not help to put the suspicions to rest. And, as much as it's hard for me to admit, there is some truth in it. But I would like you to work with us on a permanent basis."

Bramble's children flew out from underneath the desk. "No no no no," Briar said. "It's a trick!"

His sister didn't speak, she simply flew around the office, as if looking for a way out.

"SETTLE!" The word came out with more authority than Fernlight had heard from Bramble in their entire acquaintance. The two children immediately perched on the edge of the desk, both trembling.

"How can we trust you?" Fernlight asked. "You said that the reputation is valid. How do we know we will be safe?"

Mamoru cleared his throat and straightened his tie. "We have a new director. She was impressed with what you did on this case. She believes, as do I, that we cannot be successful unless we have magical folk working for us. Her preference is that you close your office and become employees. But I didn't think you would do that. So, she wishes to engage your agency as full-time consultants. You will be part of a unit that is composed of magical folk and humans. And I will be leading it, so I will expect mutual cooperation."

Fernlight looked at Bramble, but he was glaring at his children. She saw his mouth moving, so they were receiving a lecture at the fairy range of hearing. "Bramble, what do you think? It's a decision for both of us."

Bramble finished whatever he was saying, and then turned to her and Mamoru. "I have two questions before I say what I think. The first question is, who else will be part of this team from the Real Folk? And the second question is, what about Heath's murder?"

Mamoru took another envelope from his jacket. When he opened it, Fernlight saw a single sheet of paper inside. "This is a list of people that we want to recruit. I would value your opinion on them whether you join us or not."

Fernlight and Bramble looked at the list. It contained the names of two druids, a sidhe, and both Lionel and Dionne. The last two made her believe that Mamoru was sincere. They had both been involved in creating the prophecy. Dionne was one of the six, holding power in all spheres of witch magic. None of the people on the list would be intimidated, in fact it might work the other way around when the humans found out how important they were.

"Okay, these are good names. Have they said yes?" Bramble asked.

"We were hoping you would help us approach them," Mamoru said.

Bramble's children left the desk and floated over the list. Neither was more than six inches tall, but within the next year they would gain maturity. And, eventually, would replace their father as he came to the end of his life.

"We will help you," Fernlight said. "But you must accept these two children as part of the team. Bramble and I will be responsible for their training."

Bramble looked at her and grinned, all of his pointed teeth showing. "Yes, it is important that my children be trained. I will help you, as much as I can. But the sidhe won't listen to a fairy. So, I will not be involved in that. And if we join you, you will have to make sure that the sidhe does not speak down to us."

Mamoru nodded, and took the list back. "I will manage all of my team in a fair manner. And as to Heath's murder, that will be our first case."

Fernlight noticed that he didn't say they would be part of that investigation even if they didn't agree to join HOP-D. She looked at Bramble; this was a good opportunity for them, but it meant that their business would only have one client. And that was dangerous for business. Bramble simply nodded at her.

"We agree to work with HOP-D," she said. "We will not be exclusive, but you will be our priority client. I cannot jeopardize the future by tying it to your organization. And you will give us all authority, as if we were employees." This was the first time she had negotiated on something so large. Mamoru did not respond immediately. It might be good if he had to go back to his director. It would give them time to talk.

"Very well," he said. "We will meet your demands. Our first case starts tomorrow. We will work alone, until you can convince the others to join."

Want More?

Is the agency safe? Use the QR code to grab your copy of Ritual Magic Rock and work the team's next thrilling case.

Sneak peek next.

If you enjoyed reading Blood Magic Blues, please consider helping other readers to find the story by leaving a review.

Chapter 1

Bramble marched across the grassy lawn in front of the druid museum, his wings flat against his back to keep them under control. It was uncomfortable, but better than suddenly floating away in surprise.

Someone, probably a human, had placed a marker commemorating the people who died in this same place five years ago. Kali had owned their world then. It was better now, not perfect, but that would be boring. At least Arianrhod was willing to mind her own business and not cause trouble.

A few days ago, right after they solved their first case, he'd agreed to help find new team members for their secret department in HOP-D. Fernlight kept saying they weren't a secret, but that didn't sound like as much fun. So now instead of just Fernlight and him, the team included Lionel, the wizard who'd helped save the world, and a human named Kim Price who wasn't like other humans. She didn't scare him or his children. She had red hair and the sidhe did too, so maybe she was a bit magical. He hoped she didn't turn out to be as mean as the sidhe. So far, she was the only human on the team. Mamoru didn't count because he thought he was the boss.

He didn't understand why they needed to waste time looking for partners. They should be out finding Heath's murderer; it had been at least three days — an age for a fairy. It did make him feel important and proud to be talking to a druid about investigating — and a bit scared.

Fernlight said they needed a druid on the team because they were very wise. Bramble was here to talk to one and convince him to join them. Although why anyone would say no was a mystery to him. It was important to do this work. And if he was successful, they could start hunting Heath's killer. And he must remember they were making sure HOP-D stood for all people, not just humans. That's why they named it Human Occult Protection Department. Of course, humans acted like they were as short-lived as fairies and didn't take the time to say the whole name.

He sat in the middle of the grass and waited. Going into the museum felt a little daunting, and Rhodri had said he would meet Bramble outside. That was better, and a good sign. He knew enough about fairies to be considerate.

Bramble watched the big door open and a druid step out. Now that it was time, Bramble started to worry. Did Archdruid Trahaearn make sure all the vampires were in the prison of the Gur amulet? They'd possessed the druids for many lifetimes; could one of them have survived?

His body trembled and he stood, curling his toes into the grass to keep from floating up. "Don't be stupid," he told himself.

Rhodri looked very much like a human, but Bramble saw the glow of magic around him from casting spells just before coming out. No one really cared about glowing anymore.

He felt the trembles start again. "You must be brave," he whispered to himself. "This is not the way a king behaves."

The druid took his time crossing the lawn. He lowered his

hood so Bramble could see he was smiling, and he wasn't angry. And no vampire spirit shone from his green eyes.

"King Bramble," Rhodri said, giving a shallow bow. "It is a pleasure to meet with you."

"Yes," Bramble said. "Will you join our team?" *That was too fast!*

"Perhaps. I have permission from Trahaearn to make my own choice. The grove is as healed as it can be from the vampire atrocity. He can spare one of us to help with a good cause."

"Good." Relief calmed Bramble as he saw how easy it was to recruit people. "Let's go."

Rhodri didn't move. "Please, sit and talk to me about this opportunity. I have not yet decided." He lowered himself to the grass and patted the ground when Bramble didn't join him.

"Why would you say no?" Bramble stepped forward. "This is important work."

"Sit with me." Rhodri patted the ground again.

Bramble plunked down on the grass. "What do you want to talk about?" He didn't want to hang around talking to a druid. Heath's murder needed investigating. Bramble was not going to let anyone do that without him.

"I know nothing about the team. A human named Mamoru spoke to my archdruid about the possibility but gave us no details."

They should have told me that.

The stories bubbled up inside him, but Bramble had learned to control his enthusiasm. People had difficulty following him, and Fernlight said she was tired of pointing out that he was in the 'only fairies can hear you' range. He needed a little time to organize his thoughts. "Why do you want to leave the museum?"

"That is a good question," Rhodri said. "I was beginning to feel like you didn't care."

Bramble stopped listening to his inner voice and paid attention to what the druid said. "Of course we do."

"That is good to hear." Rhodri picked at his robes as he continued. "The grove is settled. I find myself in need of a challenge, and Trahaearn is not yet ready for us to seek out new knowledge. And I believe that the old ways are fading, and we need to be more flexible."

"Then you will like what we do," Bramble said. He didn't get too many chances to just talk. Maybe Fernlight was wrong about needing to filter his words. "We recently solved the case of the Blue Man. That's what I call it, anyway. Mamoru has a series of numbers and letters. A human tried to make a drug that would give him magic. When I say tried, I guess he did it. But it was deadly to him. We made sure it was destroyed. We haven't gotten a new case yet... except we do have a case. You know that Heath was murdered. We are going to find the people who did it. He was working with mysterious humans and that's where we'll start." He took a breath and remembered Rhodri wanted to learn new things. "And we search for things on the Internet. I find it extremely useful in teaching us how to speak to humans. They require a lot of reassurance for such large creatures."

Rhodri held up his hand. "Thank you for that. Will all our cases be about magical folk?"

Bramble blinked. Why did it seem like everyone had questions he never thought of? "I don't know. We are supposed to be helping HOP-D become more friendly to our kind. But that might not happen if we only do cases about magic problems. We can ask Mamoru together if you join us." Bramble pressed his lips together to stop more words from escaping.

"I do not wish to work in the HOP-D offices," Rhodri said.

"No one wants that!" Bramble beamed. This was easy to deal with. "It's a big building and so far from the ground. We work out of our business offices. Fernlight and I are private detectives."

Rhodri stood. "I think we should go there," he said.

"You will be happy with your decision. Do you like children?" Bramble walked toward the trees as he continued speaking. "My children, Briar and Thistle, work with us. They are training to be part of our team."

Is the agency safe? Use the QR code to grab your copy of Ritual Magic Rock and work the team's next thrilling case.

Free ebook

Claim your copy of Spells and Other Charms when you use the QR code to sign up for my newsletter and learn more about Quinn and Cate's past.

Also by P A Wilson

For more books by P A Wilson

Use the QR code below or go to pawilson.ca

About the Author

Perry Wilson is a Canadian author based in Vancouver, BC who has big ideas and an itch to tell stories. Having spent some time on university, a career, and life in general, she returned to writing in 2008 and hasn't looked back since (well, maybe a little, but only while parallel parking).

She is a member of the Vancouver Writers Social Group, The Royal City Literary Arts Society, and The Surrey Writing Workshop. Perry has self-published several novels. She writes the Madeline Journeys, a fantasy series about a high-powered lawyer who finds herself trapped in a magical world, the Quinn Larson Quests, which follows the adventures of a wizard named Quinn who must contend with volatile fae in the heart of Vancouver, and the Charity Deacon Investigations, a mystery thriller series about a private eye who tends to fall into serious trouble with her cases, and The Riverton Romances, a series based in a small town in Oregon, one of her favorite states. Her stand-alone novels are Breaking the Bonds, Closing the Circle, and The Dragon at The Edge of The Map.

For more information
www.pawilson.ca
pawilson@pawilson.ca

Acknowledgments

People think that the process of writing is solitary. That's not the case for me. I have help from so many people it would be hard to acknowledge everyone, but I'll give it a try.

The support and inspiration I get from my writer's groups is incalculable. The Vancouver Writers Social Group opens my mind to other ways of telling a story. The Royal City Literary Arts Society gives me the opportunity to meet and share with other writers who have more knowledge than I do. The Other 11 Months group is where I learn about getting the words on the page. And my critique group who helps me find the best parts of the story I want to tell. Thanks to all of the members of these great groups.

Last of all, but definitely a huge part of the process, my beta readers. These are the people who love stories and are willing, and more than able, to tell me if my finished story is ready for you, my readers.